A CARL TATUM MYSTERY

TIN HOLLOW

ALSO BY
J.B. HOGAN

A CARL TATUM MYSTERY

TIN HOLLOW

J.B. HOGAN

SHANNON PRESS

AN IMPRINT OF
OGHMA CREATIVE MEDIA

ISBN: 978-1-63373-168-4

Interior Design by Casey W. Cowan
Editing by George "Clay" Mitchell

Shannon Press
Oghma Creative Media
Fayetteville, Arkansas
www.oghmacreative.com

AUTHOR'S NOTE

I want to thank Casey Cowan, George "Clay" Mitchell, and Gordon Bonnet of Oghma Creative Media for their help in bringing this book to fruition. I also want to give special thanks to Casey for the incredible—and incredibly well-received—cover. Oghma wants the Carl Tatum mystery train to keep on rolling, and so after we write its sequel, tentatively titled *Bringing Down the House*, George "Clay" Mitchell will inherit the series and put his considerable skills and creativity to the task of continuing Carl's story. Stick around, things are just beginning to heat up.

—J.B. Hogan
Fayetteville, Arkansas
August 18, 2016

IN BACK OF THE ALLEY

In the opaque blackness of pre-dawn on an August Saturday morning in 1935, a three-quarter moon shone down from behind thin, drifting clouds, occasionally illuminating the darkest corners of a silent, littered back alley in the poorest part of poor Jefferson, Arkansas.

As the clouds drifted through the ending night, the moon appeared briefly and a stream of light revealed an awkwardly positioned, elongated form at the back of the alley. Motionless, the form lay beside a metal trash can standing by a discarded axle from some rusted out and long since scrapped vehicle. A light breeze moved through the alley tossing bits of scrap paper here and there. There was no sound save the rustling of the wind.

In the adjacent block, a sudden noise broke the quiet of the dying night. The back door of a late-closing hole in the wall bar and grill creaked open and a shaft of soft yellow light briefly lit the empty street as an elderly black man stepped into the street with two sacks of garbage. The door swung back shut behind him, and he peered warily in both directions, as if there might be some unseen activity there in the silent dark.

In a moment, apparently satisfied that he was alone, the man slowly walked several quiet steps down the street and turned to his left into the dirt alley. Just before he reached the trash can by the old axle, the moon again shone in the alley and the man saw the dark, motionless form. He stopped instantly. There was something familiar about the shape of the form, something that triggered the man's instinctive sense of caution and self-preservation.

"Oh, my. What's this?"

Dropping the bags of garbage, he took a very careful step forward. The form was what he feared it would be. It was definitely that of a man, lying face down, not moving.

"Oh, Lord." He stopped himself with a hand over his mouth. Looking around the alley fearfully, he knelt briefly beside the body. "Lord have mercy!"

Rising and taking to his heels, the old man rushed back down the alley, away from the body. He did not look back.

AT THE FAIRGROUNDS BALLPARK

Fred Casey, long-suffering manager of the home-standing Jefferson Redbirds, had called in his ballplayers for an unusual pre-game talk. The Redbirds, dead last in the standings, were playing an early-starting game against the Cassville Bears, one of their rivals in the Ozark Mountain League, a tiny, obscure Class D minor league struggling, like the rest of the country, to survive during the heart of the Great Depression. As he prepared to address his charges from the end of the third base dugout closest to home plate, Fred rocked back and forth on his hopelessly dirty and worn out baseball cleats.

"This ain't funny, boys," Fred told his batch of misfit city kids, country boys, and local would-be athletes. "Who knows where Cooper is? Rucker, you coverin' for 'im again?"

Jack Rucker, a tall lanky first baseman, looked away from the manager when he answered. "No, sir, Fred—er, Coach Casey. I ain't seen Ace nowheres."

"What about the rest of you?" Fred gave Rucker a harsh glare. Rucker and Cooper were thick as thieves, the veteran manager knew, and Rucker was just as likely to lie to protect Ace as he was to make a really fine play in the field—both of which events occurred pretty often.

After a lot of shuffling and some mumbling among the players, a short, scrawny little utility player, Artie Calvin, finally and timidly raised his hand. Fred shifted his glare to the useful but annoying backup man.

"Well, Calvin, what is it?" He liked to seem tough to the boys. They gave you less guff that way. They were bad enough even with that. What with their running around, drinking moonshine, and chasing local girls, sometimes Fred thought he was running a home for wayward boys instead of a professional ballclub. Professional so to speak. "I guess you wanna start in place of Cooper? Is that right?"

"Uh, yes—I mean, no sir, skipper. I was just gonna say that Ace's girlfriend Wanda is back there in the bleachers." He jerked his thumb in the direction of the seats in back of the dugout. "Reckon she might have some idee."

"Well, thank you, Sherlock," Fred said, causing general laughter in the dugout. "As if anybody in the world could miss Wanda Jeter." Fred shook his head. There were a few more snickers.

Before Fred could get back to the business at hand, Jake Hand, a one-armed umpire who'd been working the Ozark Mountain League during both years of its brief existence, walked over to the dugout to get the Redbirds out onto the field.

"Fred," Hand called out, "Fred Casey." Fred turned away from his boys to address the ump.

"What is it, Jake?"

"Ten-thirty, Fred. Time to play ball. You boys don't mind takin' the field, do you? Cassville has another game at two-thirty up in Siloam. You want to get your boys on the field? Now come on."

Sighing deeply as the umpire strolled back to home plate, Fred clapped his hands and waved his boys out of the dugout. He would have to find out where his star player was from somebody else.

"All right, fellows," Fred called to his charges with a resignation born of years dealing with minor league ballplayers in forgotten minor league towns in obscure minor leagues all around the nation, "take the field. Draper, switch over to Ace's slot at third. Calvin, get your scrawny butt out to second base."

Draper, the short, stocky, and usual starting second baseman trotted over to third. Calvin charged out onto the field like a soldier taking an enemy hill.

"Hot dog!" He raced out to take second. "Yee ha!"

In the dugout Fred lowered his head and stared at his feet. There was nothing you could do about these boys.

At home, Jake Hand was bent over brushing dirt off the plate. As Calvin rushed by to take his position, he swooped down and gave the one-armed arbiter a swat on the rear with his ragged, threadbare second sacker's glove. Hand popped up with his equally threadbare whiskbroom and waved it at Calvin.

"You watch your business there, mister," Hand called to the happy ballplayer. Laughing, but running on, Calvin cried back at the ump in a singsong voice.

"Two blind mice, two blind mice."

The field umpire, an older man from up in Missouri known only by his last name of Skelton, shook his head and moved into position behind first base. Back in the Redbirds dugout, Fred Casey handed a scorecard to a player and stepped out onto the hard ground of the fairgrounds ballfield. He slowly surveyed the rough, dirt infield; the outfield with the grass needing a mowing even though it was browning under the hot summer sun.

The outfield was bordered by a wooden fence with fading ads for local businesses, few of whom saw fit to actually support their local team, the lowly Redbirds. Slowly, then, inexorably, Fred's gaze drifted away from the field, to his left; then further behind to the wooden bleachers, which always needed painting, to the shapely form of lovely, red-headed Wanda Jeter.

Wanda appeared to be looking for someone herself—no doubt the missing Robert "Ace" Cooper, her current beau. Instinctively she felt Fred's eyes alight on her but she did not look back. Instead, she unselfconsciously adjusted her padded seat on the bleachers and with a slender arm and hand and thin graceful fingers straightened a wrinkle in her dress. The stylishly sensual gesture was not lost on Fred, who whistled under his breath.

"Lordy, lordy. What a gal."

BACK IN THE ALLEY

Jefferson Police Chief Ned Patton and Patrolman Roy Holmes, both dressed in crisply pressed and starched uniforms with dark brown patches on the upper shoulders of their light brown shirts and dark brown stripes down the sides of their light brown pants, stood beside the body of the dead man discovered earlier in the morning. Behind the policemen and off to one side were the old black man who found the body and a black woman, Ola Mae Eddin, owner of the café and bar establishment where the gray-haired, slightly stooped old man worked as dishwasher, stockman, and garbage dumper.

"Who found this here?" Chief Patton removed his tall, square-billed policeman's cap and wiped his brow. It was still early in the day but it was going to get hot fast.

"Dinty Blaine there found him, chief," Holmes said, pointing to the old black man. Dinty hunched his once wide, strong shoulders as if he didn't really want to be considered the main source of the find.

"That's right, chief." Ola Mae added more discomfort to Dinty's already troubled state. "It was Dinty here found him. Ain't that right, Dinty."

Dinty nodded weakly. "Hmm."

Dinty was fifty-eight years old. He was born right after reconstruction days of parents who had both been slaves. Jefferson was not one of the more vicious southern towns—it had had a nearly fifty-fifty split between unionists and confederates during the great war—but Dinty had been raised in a time when black folks stayed the heck right out of white folks' problems. His daddy and momma had taught him that and although he had worked for nearly every white person in Jefferson at some time or another and everyone in town knew him and liked him, Dinty believed firmly in keeping to his side of town.

Despite the vast and sweeping progressive social changes brought in by the Roosevelt administration—mostly whispers and rumors in this neck of the woods—Dinty was not one to mix himself up in other folks' problems. All this equality for colored people he'd been hearing about that was supposed to be going on in places like New York, St. Louis, and even Little Rock—well, that could be happening in some foreign land for all he knew. Dinty, who was nothing if he wasn't old-fashioned, stuck to his guns. He stayed as far from trouble as he could get, especially of the lighter-skinned variety. This darned dead white man, however, was making that philosophy a hard thing to follow.

"We know who this is yet, Holmes?"

"We pretty sure he's Somebody Cooper." Holmes tapped the body with a dusty boot. "Plays for the Redbirds."

"Redbirds?"

"You know, Chief." Holmes felt good that he knew something the chief didn't, "that team plays out at the fairgrounds. Started up last summer."

"Ain't got much time for baseball." The chief burst Holmes's little momentary bubble of superiority.

"No, sir." He looked over at Ola Mae and Dinty and frowned. Neither one returned the patrolman's attention.

"How you know he's who you say he is, Somebody Cooper?"

Holmes shrugged. "Ola Mae there says he used to come around late nights."

"Here in Tin Holler?" Chief Patton said incredulously. "With all the shines?"

"He's dead here among 'em, ain't he?" Holmes asked bluntly, rashly. He hurried to correct his attitude. "I mean—well, this here is where the body was found, sir."

"Call that boy over here that found him." Patton sneered. He was used to commanding in Jefferson—the town he considered, and to some degree rightly so, as his own private fiefdom. Holmes dutifully signaled to Dinty Blaine, who reluctantly stepped away from Ola Mae and approached the two white policemen.

"I know you, Dinty Blaine." The chief looked the short, older man over carefully. "Ola Mae lettin' you work for her these days, huh?"

"Yes, sir," Dinty admitted.

"Well, Dinty, tell me now. How come it is you wait what, most half a day to tell anybody about this dead white man?"

Dinty rocked from side to side and considered an answer. "Wadn't none of my concern, Mr. Chief."

Holmes snorted. "You figure it was white folks trouble, did you?"

"Yes, chief, sir. That's exactly what I was figurin'."

"Even here by the holler?" The chief grinned. "It don't seem funny to you a white man dead over here?" Dinty was silent. "All right. Go on, then."

Dinty stepped back behind Ola Mae.

The chief turned his attention to the bar owner. "How about you, Ola Mae? You hear anything?"

"No, sir!" She waved a hand in the air for emphasis.

"You ever see this boy before?" She was slow answering. The chief crossed his arms over his chest. "Come on, now, Ola Mae, I know some white folks come to your place late night. It ain't a complete secret."

"Well, sir." She said it as if that was enough.

"He a regular? Liked him some dark meat did he?" Ola Mae looked away. "Dinty?"

Dinty peaked over the woman's shoulder. "He come sometimes. I seen him."

Ola Mae gave her employee a strong look. The old man looked away.

Holmes rolled his eyes. "I figure it for some crazy out of town nigra."

The patrolman was never too clear on when and where he should or should not speak to the chief. As usual, he made the wrong choice.

"Oh, do you now, Mr. Dick Tracy?" Chief Patton liked to make ironic references to Dick Tracy; it showed he was up on the latest comics in the newspaper. It not only seemed to impress whoever he was speaking to of late, but made his wife *and* his girlfriend laugh at his wit as well. The chief thought of himself as quite a character.

"Our colored people don't kill no white people." Holmes gulped, eyes darting from side to side. Whenever the chief used that frosty, sarcastic tone of voice, it meant trouble for whomever it was aimed at.

Like most citizens of Jefferson, Holmes was just plain afraid of Police Chief Ned Patton. Even though Patton was currently under federal indictment down in Fort Smith for running illegal alcohol, consorting with women of questionable repute, eliminating an enemy or two—though no one ever knew where those enemies went to after the chief turned his attention to them—and allowing—if not openly running—a local car theft ring, Patton was still The Man in Jefferson, and he intended to do his level best to stay that way, Clean Government League be damned. He took no guff from anyone—especially some small-fry patrolman who didn't know how to keep his mouth shut.

"Holmes, go pick up Floyd Meadows."

Holmes demonstrated again just why he would never get anywhere in the Jefferson Police Department. "Floyd Meadows? That crazy damned boot? Why he couldn't...."

Patton turned a baleful gaze on his partolman, and Holmes shut up.

"Do I need to remind you—*yet again*—just who the chief of this department is, *Officer* Holmes?"

The patrolman's eyes grew wide. "Yes, sir. I—I mean, no, sir. Sorry, sir."

"Then kindly do as you've been told and bring me Floyd Meadows."

"Yes, sir." Holmes turned to go, but then, as befitted his poor decision making in general, stopped. "What you gonna do, chief? You gonna arrest Floyd? You gonna put this on him?"

"If it's any of your damned concern, Holmes, I'm going to get Doc Pearson to start trying to find out why this Cooper fellow died. Then I believe I'll run out to the fairgrounds. Maybe your baseball buddies will have some idea what this is all about."

"Oh." Chastised, Holmes spun on his heel and scurried away, muttering under his breath. "I never get to do nothin' interestin'. Same old crap ever time."

BACK OUT AT THE BALLPARK

The game between the Jefferson Redbirds and the Cassville Bears had reached the top of the third inning by the time Chief Patton, who actually liked baseball but never got to watch it because he was so busy keeping his underlings in line and fighting off the local legal system that seemed so intent on removing him from office, reached the ballpark.

Walking towards the field, the chief could see that Cassville had mounted a rally of sorts, with men on second and third base. The Cassville hitter, a left-handed giant of a man that someone in the crowd cheered on as "Buzz," waited at the plate. In the Redbirds dugout, or what passed as one, Fred Casey intently watched the action on the field and did not at first hear his name called out.

"Fred!" The voice carried above the chattering of nearby fans, "Fred Casey."

Finally, Fred heard the voice and slowly turned around in its direction. To his surprise, and some dread, there was Chief Patton, whom Fred knew vaguely—only enough to know the man was usually either trouble himself or the bearer of word about such trouble. Fred walked slowly back to the fence and faced the chief.

"What can I do for you, chief?"

"Fred." The chief gave him a disarming smile. "I have some items here I need for you to take a look at."

"Me?"

"We found a fellow early this mornin' down in the colored section of town and word is he might be one of your'n."

"Mine?"

"Take a look at this stuff." The chief held some items out for Fred to see.

Among them were a worn, leather billfold, a key chain, and a letter of some sort. Fred's suddenly ashen face was all the confirmation Chief Patton needed.

"Robert 'Ace' Cooper's?"

Fred nodded in the affirmative.

"Definitely belonged to your boy?"

"Yes." The manager's voice was barely above a whisper.

"I understand he had a girlfriend. That Wanda Jeter I believe."

Fred nodded his head towards the bleachers behind and to the chief's right. "Back there. Where she always sits."

"Oh, yes." The chief's eyes cut that way. "Don't know how I managed to miss that. Must be gettin' old, huh?" He laughed.

The chief's attempt at humor was lost on Fred, for the veteran manager was deep in thought, already trying to figure out a way to tell his boys about the loss of their teammate. It would hit them hard—especially Rucker He'd been Ace's best buddy on the club. And the girl Wanda, surely it would devastate her, even if she did have a reputation for being a high-powered, fast-moving woman.

The chief, through with Fred, walked the few steps to the bleachers and climbed several rows to where Wanda sat. She made no sign that she noticed him coming up the stands towards her.

When Chief Patton was beside the woman, he stopped and doffed his cap. "Miss Wanda Jeter?"

"Yes?" Wanda put a hand up to block the sun from her view of the chief. "Well, for heaven's sake, Chief Patton. Y'all don't have to be so formal with me. I know who you are. You know me."

"Well, Wanda, I appreciate that. I do know you, of course, but I'm on official business here today."

"Official business, here? With me?"

Wanda was a naturally flirtatious girl, and it showed. Chief Patton had to concentrate to remember the seriousness of his mission. "Miss Wanda. I'm sorry to say, but I may have some bad news for you."

"Bad news, why whatever could be bad …." Her smile disappeared and she fidgeted in her seat.

"Could you identify these items I have here, miss, please?" The chief presented the same items he had to Fred Casey moments before. "I showed 'em to Fred down there and he was pretty sure they belonged to a ballplayer fellow name of Robert 'Ace' Cooper, a … uh, good friend of yours I understand."

Wanda looked away momentarily from the things the chief held and down to the Redbirds dugout. Fred Casey stood there, motionless, leaning forlornly against the fence. Then Wanda looked again at the billfold, key chain, and letter. Her face, though perhaps slightly whiter than when the chief first approached her, betrayed little of her reaction to the items the chief continued to present to her.

"Robert and I were friends, that's true."

"This letter here is addressed to you. You were just friends?"

"We saw one another on social occasions from time to time."

She didn't seem as upset, the chief thought, about the probability of this Ace boy being dead as old Fred had. A cool bird, this one.

"Social occasions as in being boyfriend and girlfriend?"

"That's a personal matter."

"Well, there's one more personal matter I need for you to attend to on behalf of Mr. Cooper."

"What is that, sir?"

Patton jerked a thumb over his shoulder, back in the general direction of town. "If you would be kind enough to accompany me uptown, I would appreciate you looking at a fellow was found in an alley out at the edge of Tin Hollow this morning."

Wanda noticeably caught her breath. So there was some feeling there, the chief took note.

"Tin Hollow?"

"Yes."

"Why in that place? Why me?"

"The first one we don't know yet, honestly. As for the second... Wanda, you appear to have been the closest person to him off the ballfield. You'll know if it's Ace Cooper or not."

With a sigh, Wanda wobbled to an upright position on her four-inch red high heels. Just as she attempted to stand, with the chief reaching out his right hand to assist her, out on the field, a big Cassville hitter caught a weak roundhouse curveball from the Jefferson pitcher and with a long, powerful swing deposited it well beyond the right field fence for a three-run homer.

Fred Casey's immediate reaction was to bolt from the Jefferson dugout and chew his pitcher out, but the recent parlay with Chief Patton had tempered the manager's combative baseball spirit, and the old baseball war horse stopped before he got to the third base line, having only stepped a few feet towards the field.

"Dang it all." He watched the big Cassville hitter trot around the bases his face lit up with a big boyish grin. "Ain't that just all we need right now? Dang it all to hell."

"What's the matter, Fred?" The big man laughed as he rounded third base with a whoop.

"Dang you, too, Buzz Allen. You big old pain in the rear."

Allen, who was by far the favorite player in the Ozark Mountain League, even in enemy ballparks—to say nothing of its best hitter—absolutely ate up Redbirds pitching—as he did most of the pitching on the other teams as well. The powerful first sacker waved happily at Fred as he jogged down the third base line towards home.

"Get on home," Fred called after him. "Quit hot doggin' and get on to your dugout and stop showing off, you big lummox."

"See ya, Fred," Allen doffed his cap in mock courtesy to the Jefferson manager, players, and crowd. A few fans sent good-natured catcalls out Allen's way. At home, he made a show of touching the dirty plate and shook the offered hand of the Cassville on-deck hitter.

Back by third, Fred Casey took his cap off, wiped his brow with the sleeve of his dusty uniform, turned and just headed back to the Redbirds dugout. There wasn't anything he could do about anything anyway.

AT THE CITY MORGUE

Chief Patton and Wanda Jeter stood on one side of a metal hospital gurney in the city morgue while Arthur "Doc" Pearson was on the other, a medical transcriber to the doctor's left, pad at the ready.

"This is not likely to be very pleasant, Miss Jeter." The doctor looked down kindly at the pretty young woman who had been drug there against her will for the sole purpose of determining whether the man in the Jefferson city morgue was her ballplaying boyfriend Ace Cooper.

The body was covered with a white sheet dotted with dark red stains, either from wounds or the doctor's previous investigations. Wanda could barely look at the sheet, much less at what might be lying underneath it. Chief Patton gave Doc Pearson a nod and the medical man pulled the sheet down and off the corpse's face.

With a little gasping sound, Wanda caught her breath. It was an odd sound she emitted, the others thought, perhaps borne as much from thrill as from shock.

Chief Patton was all business. "Is this him? Is this your Robert "Ace" Cooper?"

"Yes." Wanda's voice was barely audible. "Yes, sir. It's—it's him."

"Yes?" The chief leaned in toward her. "Did I hear you say yes?"

"Yes." Wanda turned away from the body, covering her mouth with her hand. "Yes, it's him."

"When did you see him last?"

Wanda turned and looked at him with hurt eyes.

The chief was not impressed. "When?"

"At yesterday's game." She straightened her shoulders and made an effort to regather her composure.

Patton gave her no quarter. "That was the last time. Not after?"

"No."

She appeared miffed by the chief's questions, and he liked it. "You and the deceased have a fight or anything?"

Wanda gave him a haughty look. "Robert and I never quarreled."

"Robert was it?" The chief smirked, his trademark sarcasm evident for all to hear. "Never quarreled?"

"*Never.*"

"Well, hush my mouth." The chief looked around the room for approval, which he only got from Doc Pearson, who managed a weak smile. "Don't sound like me and my old woman."

Wanda looked down at her stylish shoes. The medical transcriber by the door scratched the back of his neck.

Patton turned sober. "You have any idea why he would have been found over there in coon holler?"

Wanda crossed her arms. "How could I?"

She was definitely offended now, no doubt about it. She absolutely did not appreciate herself or her late boyfriend being associated with 'that' side of town.

"I'm sure I wouldn't know anything about such things. Robert and I knew very well where we belonged in Jefferson."

"Uh-huh." The chief grunted, extracting a fat, cheap cigar from his uniform shirt pocket and depositing it in the corner of his mouth. Doc Pearson wagged a finger at the chief.

"Sorry, Chief, can't smoke that in here. Too many chemicals. We'd go up like a roman candle."

"Just plannin' to chew it, Doc. Don't go to frettin'."

"Sure. I wasn't frettin', Chief, just wanted to let you know. That's all."

The chief ignored him, keeping his gaze on Miss Wanda.

"You know if he went there a lot?"

Wanda examined a well-trimmed, red-painted fingernail. She'd become bored with this entire line of questioning. Maybe she had other things to do—more important than hanging out with a corpse in a sterile old morgue. "Where?"

"Tin Hollow." Patton was getting a little annoyed himself. "Where we found his dead body, dammit."

She sighed. "You needn't get angry with me, Chief Patton. I told you no already. I can't believe Robert would ever go to such a place. We certainly never did together."

"Well, Miss Jeter, he did." The policeman pressed on. "You broke up pretty bad about the deceased?"

"We were friends." Wanda chose to ignore the chief's continuing tone of sarcasm. "That's all."

"Now, I hear tell he was your beau."

"We were friends."

"All right, then." The chief concluded his questioning by releasing a big breath of air. He was satisfied the young woman—deluded as she might be about Ace Cooper—had had nothing to do with his demise. "That's enough for now. I'll leave you to your grievin'."

She glared at him icily. "May I go now?"

"Go right on." Patton have her a big, insincere smile. "But be around in case I need to talk to you again. Understand?"

Without answering the chief's last question, Wanda Jeter turned on her shapely feet and walked silently out of the morgue. The men watched her go; watched the natural swishing movement of her hips from side to side. Wanda Jeter was a good looking woman whether she was mad, happy, or indifferent. It was a natural condition; nothing she could do anything about. But, each man thought, she was as cool as a cucumber in a dark country cellar.

"Whew." Doc Pearson whistled. "Colder than the morgue itself, and a hundred times finer."

A laugh. "At least. At least."

The doctor shook his head. "My, oh my. What a fine lookin' filly."

"Uh-huh." The chief sighed. He turned back toward the body on the gurney. Time to get down to the business of determining the cause of death for one Robert "Ace" Cooper. "This old boy looks pretty bad beat, Doc. Whad'ya think killed him?"

"He was beaten severely." Doc Pearson motioned toward the purple splotches marking Cooper's torso and upper body. "Bruises on the forehead, neck, side of the head. His right hand is broken. But those knife wounds killed him. Probably your average knife, not a razor like you might expect over in Tin Hollow. Probably something as mundane as a Barlow."

"How long's he been dead you reckon?"

"I estimate he had been dead six, maybe eight, hours before he was found." Doc dropped a bloodied instrument into a silver metal tray. The transcriber busily took notes.

"Last night then?"

Doc continued his examination. "Yes. Do you have any suspects yet?"

"I take it for a colored killing."

"In Jefferson?" The physician raised an eyebrow. "I can't believe any of our folks would do such a thing. Not here in Jefferson. Our worlds are separate that's true, but we've always had a cordial relationship. This isn't cotton country around here."

Chief Patton snorted. "Well, regardless of all that, it remains to be seen. I'm leanin' towards a local."

"I guess if you say so." Doc shook his head. "You're the crime expert, after all. But it sure would surprise me if it was one of our own."

"It does stand to some reason though."

Even though the autocratic chief didn't have to defend anything he did to anyone—except the city council and the district court when they were after his job—he respected Doc Pearson and wanted him on his side.

"How's that, Chief?"

"Well, for one thing. It appears this Cooper fellow was a regular over in Tin Holler. Not just somebody who might have ended up there after some kind of fight or something."

"An out of town boy, then, I would presume."

"Some kind of baseball player." Patton closed his notebook with a loud snap. "From up north somewheres. Illinois, I think it was. Maybe they more used to mixin' with one another than we are."

Pearson shrugged. "Still. We never had any trouble like that before. Not between the races. It's not like that here in Jefferson. We're a quiet little town, mostly. Except that time the Barrow gang came through."

Chief Patton cleared his throat and looked away. "I guess we'll see."

IN THE POLICE STATION

Ned Patton sat at his big police chief's desk puffing on a big, cheap cigar. The foul blue smoke drifted through the room, blown here and there by a small oscillating fan the chief had sitting on top of a nearby filing cabinet. In mid-puff there was a rapping on the door.

"Come in." The chief's voice was gruff. He hated being interrupted when he was enjoying one of his cigars. He especially hated it when the interruption turned out to be a useless patrolman like Roy Holmes. The door opened and Holmes entered the room.

The chief sighed and kept puffing on his cigar.

Slowly walking up to the desk, Holmes stood before his boss without saying a word. Impressed by his own prescience at Holmes being the one responsible for the interruption, Patton looked his subordinate over for a moment before speaking.

"Well?"

"Well?" Holmes blinked in confusion.

"Well, Holmes." The chief fought the urge to jump over the desk and bash in the patrolman's brains. "What is it?"

"Sir?"

The chief rolled his eyes in annoyance. "I don't see nobody with you. You got Floyd out in the car or somethin'? Maybe in your pocket?"

"I couldn't find him."

"No? Couldn't find him? Couldn't find goddamned useless Floyd Meadows in goddamned Jefferson, Arkansas?" Patton never swore so virulently, except for Holmes's benefit and edification.

"No, sir."

"How many people live in Jefferson, Holmes? What do you figure?"

"Shoot, Chief. I don't know."

"Don't know. Don't know. Well, for your information, there's about sixty-three hundred souls, according to the last census."

"Sixty-three hundred souls. Oh."

"How many of those you reckon are colored folks, Holmes?"

"Sir, I couldn't say exactly."

"Guess."

"Maybe a thousand?"

"Lord, Holmes, you are out of touch—or you flunked math. Remind me again why I hired you? Wait... don't answer that." Holmes started to answer but the chief raised a finger to stop him. The chief paused to take a deep, satisfying drag off his cigar. "There are, Patrolman Holmes, four hundred and forty-seven Negroes that live in Jefferson, at last count. What did you think we was, Little Rock?"

"I didn't know, sir."

"No, you didn't. But all you had to do was find one person—poor, stupid old Floyd Meadows out of four hundred and forty-seven colored people— maybe two hundred and twenty... well, two hundred twenty whatever black men and you couldn't do it."

"I looked all over the holler, sir. Couldn't find 'im."

"Went to his house?"

"Uh-huh. Nobody there."

"Ola Mae's?"

"Uh-huh."

"The hotel?"

"Yes, sir."

"Ask anybody?"

"Yes, sir. Ast that Preacher Jackson. Ast some kids."

"Nobody seen him?"

"No, sir."

"Well, hell." Sighing, Chief Patton tapped ash of the end of his cigar, tired of the questioning. Holmes was so stupid, he probably ran over Floyd. He was so almighty fond of driving that damned patrol car around town with the engine roaring, scaring little children, old people, and the colored folks.

Holmes jumped into the pause following the chief's harangue. "What you found out so far, chief? Was it for sure Ace Cooper the ballplayer?"

Patton took another long pull on his cigar and blew smoke out directly at Holmes. The patrolman coughed.

"It was."

"How'd you find out?"

"It was pretty simple." Chief Patton rolled his eyes again. "Showed his stuff to that Fred Casey fellow. And to his girlfriend."

"That Wanda Jeter?" Holmes grinned. "Oh, boy, is she something or what?"

"Took her up to Doc's to identify the body." The chief ignored his patrolman's prurient interest in the fashionable Miss Jeter. He was torn between keeping the information from his subordinate and showing off to Holmes that he, the chief, was in on a lot more inside stuff than Holmes, ever was, could be, or would be.

The showing off won, as it usually did with Patton.

"She said it was him all right. Didn't seem to bother her much. It wadn't exactly what I would call a tearful reunion. That gal don't seem much of one for cryin' over spilt milk. Or dead boyfriends."

"Think she was in on it?"

Patton waved it away. "Naw. No reason to. She's just a cold one, that's all."

Holmes snickered. "That kindly makes two of 'em, then."

Holmes's clever little joke didn't seem to amuse the chief much. Holmes put his serious face back on.

"That manager fellow, old Fred, uh, Casey." Chief Patton ignored his patrolman. "Now he seemed to take it pretty hard when I showed him Cooper's belongings. I suppose some of the boys on the team might take it pretty hard, too. I get the idea that this Cooper was well liked enough on the ballclub. And around town. For a Yankee and all."

"Did Doc find anything for you to go on?" For a change, the patrolman was actually making sense, sounding like a policeman a little bit.

"The fellow died from the knife wounds and not the beatin' he took. But I reckon either one would have done the job, if you ask me." Abruptly, Patton realized he'd been talking too much, even if Holmes had been acting almost like a regular human being for a change.

Enough small talk, though. Time to get back to the original topic.

The chief resumed speaking but with a far sterner tone than before. "I believe I sent you out to get old Floyd Meadows, didn't I, Officer Holmes? But I'm not seein' him. You got him stashed somewheres I should know?"

Holmes mumbled something unintelligible.

"What you say?"

"I done said I couldn't find him, chief."

"What?" Patton slapped his hand on the desk. "He holed up somewhere like John Dillinger?"

The patrolman's voice went up an octave. "He don't seem to be in the holler anywhere, chief."

The chief rubbed his chin thoughtfully. "See if you can go get that other old boy up here then. You know the one, the fellow helps us with colored problems from time to time. That smart boy, old Jesse's boy."

"You mean Carl Tatum?" Holmes moved his arms back and forth and hunching his shoulders like a little boy would do who was being upbraided by his father. "What we need him for?"

"If you cain't seem to find Floyd or he's off somewheres, maybe that Tatum boy can locate him."

"Ah..." Holmes groaned unhappily.

"Stop your belly achin,' Holmes." The chief held up an admonishing finger.

"Get back out and do some work. That is the one thing what your grandaddy promised me you could at least do now wadn't it, work? Now go on. If you couldn't come up with old Floyd, leastways maybe you can find Carl Tatum?"

"I don't like that boy. He's damned uppity, if you ast me."

"Ain't nobody askin' you." The chief glared at him. "And maybe he seems uppity to you because he's smarter than you are. Ever think of that? One thing for sure, he's a hell of a lot better educated, that's a fact."

"From some nigra college."

"You never mind about that. He figured out who done killed old Harley Brown last year, didn't he?"

Holmes sneered. "Blind, dumb luck. That's all it was. Blind, dumb luck."

"Nevertheless, you go on now and get him. Don't come back alone again."

"What if this boy gets to snoopin' a little too deep this time. He was pushin' it a bit on that Harley killing, now wadn't he? You ready for that, again?"

The chief reddened at the oblique reference to the recent corruption allegations aimed at the department by the newly formed Clean Government League. Its leader—city councilman Tommy Ball—was hell-bent to get Chief Patton and his machine out of office in Jefferson. The chief had beaten one federal charge, but no sooner had the dust cleared than Ball and his damned CGL, as the locals liked to call it, were after him again. It all kept coming back to the rumors about the chief being involved with loose women, moonshining and a stolen auto ring.

It seemed like Tommy Ball and his bunch of FDR-type do-gooders were out to destroy the chief. They'd managed to get another indictment started against him and they were pressing the issue at district court down in Fort Smith. For all that, though, Patton was optimistic about his chances. Jefferson was still his town. He still held most of the cards and he would play out his hand when the time was right. Ned Patton was not one to go down without a fight. Ball and the CGL knew that, so did Mayor Turnbull. When the final battle came, it would be a donnybrook, but Patton was ready and unafraid.

"You just get goin'." Patton broke away from his thoughts of the CGL and its ilk and back to the real world of his enjoyable, if mild, tongue lashing of the semi-useless Holmes. "I'll worry about what he finds out—if anything. He'll be up at the hotel 'bout now workin'. You bring him in straight way. Is that clear?"

Holmes acquiesced—as always. He turned and headed out to get in his prized patrol car. As he walked out of the city building he was muttering to himself. "All right. I'll go get him."

JEFFERSON

Jefferson was a poor town. It had always been poor. Founded shortly before Arkansas became a state back in 1836, and nestled on top of a hill right in the heart of the lushly green Ozark Mountains, Jefferson served mostly as a gateway, a stopping off place for folks headed west to Tulsa, south to Fort Smith, or north to Kansas City. During the civil war, its residents were split about fifty-fifty between the Union and the Confederacy with the result that Jefferson fell very shortly after the ferocious battle at nearby Pea Ridge in early 1862 and it remained in Union hands from then until the conflict ended, mercifully, in 1865.

Reconstruction had mostly bypassed Jefferson, and as a result there was no infusion of capital in the area and with no industry to speak of, the town languished. It did have a number of small businesses up on the quaint, traditionally southern town square, the centerpiece of which was a large, rectangular federal post office, built just before the stock market crash of '29. The post office stood in faux marble-columned majesty surrounded in all four cardinal directions by a colorful collection of stores and cafés, with movie theatres on the east and south sides.

But the stores mostly provided low cost goods for the town's low paid citizens and the even lower paid farmers who came in on Saturdays with what little money they could scrape together to buy the cloth, canned goods, and other items they couldn't get out in the country. There were few jobs to be had and no large businesses had sprung up in the perpetually economically-depressed little city.

Jefferson's saving grace was its university. Founded in the mid-1870s, the local university was the first land grant college in the state and somehow, despite Little Rock's size and status as the state capital and Fort Smith's central location in the flow of east-west travel and goods in the region, Jefferson managed to keep the school. Over time it became the state's school and its place as the center of Arkansas collegiate academics and athletics went unquestioned.

With the paving of Highway 71 in the early 1930s, the north-south corridor between Fort Smith and Texas further south and Kansas City to the north, Jefferson experienced a mild growth phase. By the middle of the decade, even in the heart of the Great Depression and with little to keep it afloat besides the university and the travelers who stayed in its small hotels and motor courts on their way to someplace else, it was a busy and optimistic, if still in reality mostly impoverished, little Ozark Mountain burgh.

Co-existing with that optimism, and championed by lean but hopeful local entrepreneurs, were other realities. For one, the town's black population, confined to several up and down hilly blocks to the east of the town square known officially as Tin Hollow and unofficially to most of the white population as Nigger Holler, lived in unrelenting poverty. Their houses, such as they were, were often no more than hurriedly thrown together piles of scrap wood and strips of tin—found God knew where—to keep out the rain and cold.

The black part of town had a Baptist church or two, one ramshackle grocery store, and a school that taught the children of Tin Hollow through the eighth grade. If a local student was good enough or promising enough for high school, they were either home taught or, more often, sent to schools in Pine Bluff, Little Rock, or Fort Smith to continue their education.

The second major reality about Jefferson in the first half of the 1930s was that its government, at least with regard to law enforcement, was corrupt to an extraordinary degree. Moonshiners, car thieves, bullies and shakedown artists—who bilked not only poor white and black citizens but store and restaurant owners as well—operated in town with little regard for or fear of police action against them. Ned Patton, the current chief of police and himself the son of a former chief of police, presided over Jefferson in an autocratic, highly subjective way.

Rumors abounded about Patton, and his brother Martin, the County Assessor. During 1932 and 1933, well-known outlaws and desperadoes, like local boy Charles "Pretty Boy" Floyd, Raymond Hamilton, and his sometime partners Clyde Barrow and Bonnie Parker—along with fellow gang members Buck Barrow and W.D. Jones—had passed through Jefferson more often than was generally known.

Some believed that they did more than simply pass through town, and in fact, in 1933, Buck Barrow and W. D. Jones had robbed Hale's Grocery, just a block to the west off Highway 71. The infamous gangsters absconded with all of thirty-two dollars from the poor little store and on their way back to join Bonnie and Clyde outside Fort Smith had shot and killed Marshall Henry D. Humphrey of Alma.

Jefferson had its bad side, no doubt, but like most places in the country it was primarily composed of hardworking, honest, and decent folk. For the most part its citizens lived in harmony with one another and despite the existence of apartheid-like segregation, its two races managed—on the surface—to maintain a respectable, if limited, interaction. The tone, remarkably enough it would seem, was mostly one of courtesy and politeness.

White businessmen reserved colored-only sections for black customers and black civic functions would maintain a whites-only area for any such citizens who wished to join them for a Sunday afternoon fundraiser or performance of the local black school choir. All in all Jefferson wasn't a bad town—it had its good and bad sides, but overall it was just what it seemed to be: another small southern town, like any other of its time.

AT THE OZARK HOTEL

While the day manager of the Ozark Hotel, located at the corner of Highway 71 and Main Street a long block east of the square, busied himself behind the check-in counter, Carl Tatum walked around the lobby picking up tiny bits of paper and such from the aging but nearly spotless carpet of the city's finest and newest hotel.

The Ozark was Jefferson's best. It was as plush and well-decorated as a depression-era hotel might be in a small, poor Ozark town—even if Jefferson was the region's largest city and the seat of Ozark County. While Carl went about his work, Roy Holmes entered from the street. Taking note of Holmes's arrival, he kept working, even as the patrolman approached in his usual arrogant manner.

"Carl Tatum?"

Carl, bent over collecting some tiny pieces of debris from the hotel rug, slowly straightened himself up and looked at the policeman. Both in their late twenties, they had known each other since childhood. Holmes's family lived on a dirt street at the far southeastern edge of Tin Hollow where, crossing the narrow two-lane highway leading east to the village of Elkins, many of Jefferson's poorest white families lived in near proximity to their black counterparts.

"Yes, boss?" Carl adopted a broadly sarcastic and ironic tone. It was an attitude he sometimes employed with local white folks who refused to acknowledge his level of intelligence and education. People like Roy Holmes stubbornly held to what Carl considered outdated, outmoded, and insultingly backward racial attitudes.

Carl had gone to school in the East—back where radical ideas of the intelligentsia included people of color, where people were beginning to understand that a black man, or woman, really could be equal to white people. Holmes was more than the two thousand physical miles from those ideas and his assumed—and unproven—superiority rankled Carl.

"I think I is, Chief Holmes, sir. Let me check. Yeah, I be. I be old Carl Tatum all right."

"Don't be a smart ass, boy."

Holmes had never liked Tatum. Didn't like his superior airs. Didn't like the fact that he had somehow got sent to some damned Negro college back east somewhere while he'd had to stay in crappy little Jefferson and work for bullying Ned Patton. Roy was a police officer, damn it, and he wouldn't take guff from any citizen, neither white nor black.

Especially not black.

Carl reverted to a standard English that was far more academically-trained than the average white citizen's in town. "Then stop acting like you haven't known me my entire life."

"Watch your tongue with me, Tatum, or I'll run your black ass in."

"Oh, I is dreadful sorry, boss." Carl did his field hand impression again.

"Stop talkin' that way. And stop callin' me boss."

He feigned innocence. "What do you want me to call you?"

"Sir. Or Officer Holmes. Just show some respect for your superiors."

"I always do."

Holmes either chose to ignore the subtle jibe, or just flat didn't catch it. "Chief Patton wants you to come in."

"The chief wants me to come in?"

Carl wasn't quite able to conceal his curiosity—or his fear—at a summons like this one. Chief Patton was an odd bird. Just when a person thought they had the man figured out as a no good crook, he'd do something to change your opinion of him. Like he had last year in asking for and getting Carl's help in solving the murder of Harley Brown, a local black who had gotten mixed up in moonshine trouble with a group of colored crooks out of nearby Madison County—the last remaining Negroes, now doing time in a state prison farm down by Little Rock, in what was now an all-white county.

After Harley's death and the newspaper stories that followed, Carl had had a moment of celebrity in Jefferson and hoped that it would help him get a chance at taking the state bar exam or at least some steady legal-oriented work in town but it hadn't. In a very short while, things were back to normal. He continued to work at the Ozark Hotel and continued to hope for a shot at the bar, which never seemed to be forthcoming.

"Well?" Holmes was tired of waiting.

"Uh-huh." Carl made sure to cover his previous, momentary lapse in hiding his feelings. He had trained himself, like most blacks, to always be on guard around whites, especially those in the power structure itself. "When's he say?"

"Right now, damn it."

"He say why?"

"Never mind the why. You just come on."

"I have to tell the manager."

Holmes rolled his eyes impatiently. "Tell him, then. And hustle it up."

"Yes, boss."

"Stop that." The patrolman smacked his thigh. "I told you to not say that."

Without replying, Carl walked back to the check-in counter to tell his boss he had to go to the police station. While he spoke to the manager, Holmes waited by the door, impatiently tapping his shoes on the carpet. These modern Negroes, he thought, sure are a royal pain in the ass.

AT THE BALLPARK ONCE AGAIN

The Cassville-Jefferson baseball game had ended in defeat for the local nine, 6-2, and their weary manager, Fred Casey, slowly walked from the dugout bench—where he had been sitting morosely watching his hapless charges—out toward home plate. Most of the guys knew something was up after the Jefferson police chief had visited with Fred about the top of the third inning. Then the owner of the team, Pete Henry, a local businessman, had come down to the dugout between the third and fourth and whispered something to Fred.

The old skipper had pretty much clammed up for the rest of the game, not even bothering to chew out bad plays and pitches as he did every day. Fred lived to yell at them and they lived for him to do it. Now, as the players, even a few from Cassville, and the umpires gathered around, Fred faced them and the small crowd remaining in the stands.

Removing his weathered ball cap with a tattered J on the front, Fred cleared his voice to speak. "Fellows.... ladies and gentlemen. I have some awful news to tell you all."

Calvin and Rucker and the other players on the team stood with their heads bowed. They knew something bad was coming. Fred continued.

"Folks, Chief Patton of the Jefferson police came by earlier and informed me that one of our—one of your—favorite players on the Redbirds, our dependable third baseman, Robert "Ace" Cooper has died."

An audible murmur ran through the crowd and among the ballplayers. Fred waited for the news to sink in a bit before going on.

He shuffled his feet. "It appears that Ace fell victim to foul play, though the chief is still investigating. That's all we know for now but we ask that every one of you say a prayer for Ace, and for his family back in Illinois. Lord knows it'll be hard on them to lose a loving son of such fineness of character."

Calvin and Rucker peeked at each other from their bowed head positions. Calvin could see tears welling up in his teammate's eyes. Fred spoke again.

"God bless you all and thank you for comin' out today." The old skipper sighed, his heart heavy. "I'm sure sorry to bring you such sad tidings and with not even a win to go home with."

"That's all right, Fred." Many in the crowd called out their encouragement. "We'll get 'em tomorrow."

Calvin and Rucker exchanged looks again. Rucker definitely was about to cry.

"Thank you," Fred called back to the fan. "And good day to you all. God bless."

Without another word, the old baseball man slowly turned and walked back to the Redbirds dugout, deeply moved by the loss of his star player. The remaining crowd filed out and the ballplayers walked towards their respective dugouts, speaking softly among themselves.

CARL VISITS THE POLICE STATION

As if it was the only position he ever occupied when he was in his office, Chief Patton sat at his desk chewing on the remains of a big, cheap cigar. Suddenly there was a knock at the door and Patrolman Holmes popped his head in.

"Here he is, chief." Holmes tried to push Carl Tatum into the room, but Carl resisted and entered of his own accord. The younger officer took up a position just inside the door, where he stood sulking.

Chief Patton smiled a conspiratorial "we know each other" kind of smile.

Carl didn't smile back.

"How you doin', Carl?"

"I'm all right, Chief." Carl held back, a good deal more reserved.

"That's good. That's good." Patton set his cigar down in a big Ford Motors Company ashtray on his desk. "Well, Carl boy, I won't keep you long from the hotel. I know you's busy there. But we have a little problem that I believe you can help us out with. Did Officer Holmes tell you about it?"

"No, sir." Carl might have said no even if Holmes had told him—just to get the patrolman's goat a little.

The chief gave his officer a sharp look. Holmes made as if to defend himself, moving his hands around some, but he thought better of it and remained silent.

Patton waved it away. "Well, that ain't no nevermind. It's really a simple thing. All we need you to do is find Floyd Meadows for us."

The young man stood his ground. "Why you need poor old Floyd for?"

"You don't need to worry about the *why*, Tatum." Holmes bolted from his spot beside the door and got right in Carl's face. "You just answer the chief and do it respectful."

Patton smiled paternally. "Now, Roy. Take it easy."

Holmes stepped back, his fierce gaze never leaving Carl.

The older man shuffled the papers on his desk. "Carl, we believe Floyd was mixed up in a knifing in an alley near Ola Mae's joint."

"You mean that dead white man?"

Holmes looked up at the chief as if a shock had been applied to his patrolman's badge.

The chief kept his face carefully neutral, nonplussed by Carl's unexpected knowledge of the crime in question. "News travels fast."

"It was right there in Tin Hollow. Everybody down there knows about it. But it wasn't Floyd, Chief. Floyd may not be full good in the head, but he ain't got a mean bone in his poor, slow body. Besides, he ain't even in town right now."

"What do you mean? How do you—"

The chief silenced Holmes with a slight movement of his hand.

"Floyd's down in Devil's Den working for a colored CCC crew fixin' up the park." Carl shrugged as though everybody should know it already. "He ain't even been around lately."

"How you know that?"

"I saw him get on the truck myself last week. And his cousin Dinty Blaine said he just got a postcard from him a day or so ago."

"Dinty's the one found the body," Holmes objected.

Patton gave his subordinate a look that would curdle milk. Holmes shut his mouth and moved back another step.

Carl smirked. "That's what I heard, too."

"Well, then, it weren't no Floyd did it." The chief sighed, lamenting the idiocy of Holmes and the others like him in the department. "I suppose we won't be needin' your services after all."

Carl didn't move. "Except...."

"Except?" Both Patton and Holmes looked at him curiously.

"Except you still have you a dead white man found in Tin Hollow." Carl paused, amused at the open-mouthed stares of the two white men. "And you got no idea in the world who did it."

The chief remained silent, pondering that one for a moment. "It possible he got dumped there?"

"It's possible. But nobody knows that yet. Do they?"

"You know somethin' about this we don't, Carl?" Patton's gaze turned suspicious. "If you do, spill it now. I ain't kiddin'."

The young black man smiled. "I could check around."

"Like you did on the Harley Brown thing? Don't get to thinkin' you're a real detective, Tatum. You just got lucky once."

Carl didn't go for the bait.

The chief considered the situation a bit more. "Still, there *is* the white body in Tin Hollow to account for. No denyin' that."

Holmes looked horrified. "But, Chief! It—it ain't right havin' no colored boy investigatin' a white murder."

"Keep quiet, Roy."

"But—"

"*Enough!*"

Holmes wilted under the chief's glare.

Patton turned back to Carl. "All right, Tatum. You check with your people in the holler. But don't you tell nobody what you find out, 'cept me. You understand? You go messin' with white folks, or botherin' 'em, and I haul you in. I know you're educated for a colored boy and all and I know you're the pet Negro of that snoopin' around, interferin' Clean Government League"—he snorted in disgust at the very name of the agency so bent on removing him from office—"but you walk a straight line here on this now. You got me?"

"You speak plain enough."

"Good." The chief smiled again. "Then you go on. Get outta here now. Find out what you can and bring it straight back to me. Nobody else."

Without responding, Carl turned and walked out of the office.

Holmes immediately began voicing his opinion. "Why you let that boy be part of our work?"

"You have got to be more political-like, Roy." The chief sighed, atypically taking the time to explain to the patrolman. "If Tatum learns anything useful to us, we take it for our ownselves. If he don't, nothin's hurt."

Holmes wasn't done, though. "What if he goes to Tommy Ball at that league thing? Ball's got it out for you already."

"I know that he will go to Ball. But I'll worry about the councilman. That's all just fine. It'll keep 'em all busy and off of me and my brother Martin's case. You keep that to yourself." Patton's voice was so cold, it could have frozen a good portion of the nether place that Roy Holmes had been taught he would most likely descend to when he left this veil of tears—the chief was just helping him feel like he had got there a bit early, that's all. "You hear me, boy? Not a word. Not if you expect to keep workin' for me."

"No, sir—I mean yes, sir. Chief." Holmes shifted back and forth on his feet.

"All right then." A small smile lightened the chief's features—much to Holmes's relief. "Now get on back to your patrollin' duties."

"Yes, sir." With a smart salute for the chief, the patrolman spun sharply around and hustled out of the office. The chief shook his head at the retreating figure. It was his burden, he told himself, to have to work with such incompetent people.

TOMMY BALL
AND THE CLEAN GOVERNMENT LEAGUE

Tommy Ball was a good-looking guy. He was tall and trim with dark, curly hair and had been a real bon vivant at the state university there in Jefferson—starring in both football and baseball and belonging to a prestigious mostly athlete-populated fraternity. The girls loved Tommy, with his solid, square jaw and bright, intelligent brown eyes, and he had married one of the prettiest, a cheerleader from El Dorado. The Balls settled into their own little home on the east side of Jefferson, where the older, but nicer homes were and had a small family, a girl and a boy.

Because he was the scion of a well-off and well-respected local family and because he was a very likable guy, Tommy developed the notion that he should go into public service. His first efforts at it were completely successful, getting him elected to the Jefferson City Council in 1932 by a very large majority over his rival, Martin Patton, brother of the city police chief.

Like ninety-nine percent of the locals, he was a staunch democrat—having come from a notable Jefferson family that included his father, Oliver W., who had started and willed to Tommy the family businesses. The family businesses were partnerships in Cardwell-Ball, a fine clothing store, and the Northwest Arkansas Bank, both of which were on Jefferson's busy square.

Tommy found that he had a knack for banking and so, while his younger sister Meg was involved in the clothing store, Tommy oversaw the transformation of the Northwest Arkansas Bank into the First National Bank of Jefferson during the first years of the Roosevelt Administration.

Because Mr. Roosevelt's economic policies had essentially saved Tommy's bank, making the young man a fair chunk of change for the depression, and because once in Little Rock he had met and been charmed completely by Mrs. Roosevelt, Tommy considered himself the local point man for the New Deal. He was a Roosevelt Democrat down to the ends of his wing tip shoes.

Although he and Jefferson Police Chief Ned Patton, a roughneck, classless bully in Tommy's opinion, did not get along very well from the start (it didn't help that he had thrashed the chief's brother in the '32 election), it wasn't until early in his second term in office that Councilman Ball became fully aware of the chief's autocratic, unethical, and—many people believed—illegal actions as the town's elected representative of local law and order.

Rumors were rife about the chief—that he turned a blind eye, or worse, to a local car theft gang, that he took kickbacks from area moonshiners, that he had illicit affairs with women he coerced using his authority as police chief, that his enemies moved away without leaving forwarding addresses, that he and his brother Martin might actually have direct connections to regional outlaws like Pretty Boy Floyd and the notorious killers Bonnie and Clyde.

In 1934, after two members of the Barrow gang actually robbed a tiny Jefferson grocery story just off Highway 71 south—later killing an Alma, Arkansas constable in their reckless getaway—Tommy and a handful of other Jefferson up and coming businessmen and civic leaders, including Tommy's best friend and fellow reformer Richard Lee Hudson, decided it was time to clean up the town. That meant finding a way to get Ned Patton out of office.

What Tommy and the others came up with was the Clean Government League. The league's bylaws called for honest, open, and democratic rule for the town; and for the elimination of illegal activity—in particular car theft, moonshine running, bribery, and extortion. The league brought Ned Patton up on all of these charges—he was known to consort with an ex-con named

Wade Smith who ran a questionable auto repair and body shop on the south end of town and his connection to local moonshiners, both black and white, was a foregone belief if not yet a provable fact.

Patton had won the first few battles with the league, getting one extortion case tossed out of district court in Fort Smith and successfully defeating a recall petition drive, but Tommy Ball and his followers were not yet ready to admit defeat. They wanted a clean town and the only way they would get it would be to rid it of the likes of Ned and Martin Patton and their bullying hirelings like Wade Smith. To this end, Tommy Ball and the Clean Government League dedicated themselves—from 1934 onwards.

IN THE OFFICE OF
CITY COUNCILMAN TOMMY BALL

In his continuing battle against the endemic corruption that had plagued Jefferson in recent years, City Councilman Tommy Ball kept a keen eye on local events, hoping that something might happen that would allow him and the Clean Government League he had helped found to defeat the abusive power base of city Police Chief Ned Patton.

The recent discovery of a dead white man near the edges of Tin Hollow, Jefferson's poor black section, gave Tommy pause. Maybe, just maybe, there would be something about this case that would turn on, point back to Chief Patton's involvement, either passive or active—it didn't matter which. Jefferson was normally such a quiet little town that an apparent murder, whatever the causes, sources, or suspects, might throw Patton in such a bad light that he could finally be deposed once and for all.

To this end, Tommy Ball had learned that the deceased, an out of town ballplayer on the local pro team, had had a "friend" in town, a woman with something of a reputation as a mankiller but one who might have information that would somehow lead this investigation back to where Tommy wanted it to: Chief Ned Patton.

On this fine summer morning, Councilman Ball—who was taking

valuable time off from his banking duties to do his elected civic duty—waited patiently in his office to conduct an informal interview with Wanda Jeter, girlfriend of the late ballplayer, Robert "Ace" Cooper. In the midst of going through some papers on his desk to pass the time, Tommy finally was interrupted by his secretary, Mary Evans, who stuck her head in the door to announce the arrival of Miss Jeter.

"Mr. Ball," Mary said in her usual professional manner, "Miss Jeter is here to see you."

"Thank you, Mary." Tommy knew the value of a good secretary, one who spared him much trivial work and who helped him balance his career as a city leader and bank president. As a consequence, he always treated Mary Evans with the respect she was due. "Show her in, please."

Wearing a stylish dark dress and looking her usual pretty self, Wanda Jeter slowly entered the room. Tommy Ball quickly noted—so as not to appear overly interested himself—the longish, curly red hair, the light green eyes, the full red mouth and shapely cheeks and chin, the smooth white skin, perfectly shaped breasts, narrow waist, and round hips above thin well groomed legs, only part of which showed below her demurely long dress. Tommy quickly noted this, then looked back at his papers briefly.

Wanda herself barely acknowledged Mary, and with the patented, sensual smoothing of her dress that so many men had noticed in Jefferson, sat in a chair directly in front of Councilman Ball's paper-cluttered desk. Behind Wanda, Mary made a little face, which Tommy Ball pretended he didn't see, and then went back to her desk beyond the councilman's office.

By nature Wanda Jeter was a flirtatious and sexy woman, but she was a little uncomfortable and even a bit afraid in the presence of the councilman and the power he represented on the local scene. She fidgeted around a bit in her seat as she waited for Tommy to address her.

"Thank you for coming, Miss Jeter." Tommy looked up from his paper shuffling to give the young woman a pleasant smile. He wanted her to be at ease. And, of course, men never had trouble smiling at Wanda. "We appreciate your taking the time to visit with us."

Wanda's hands fluttered nervously. "I don't know why I'm here, Mr. Ball. I've already told Chief Patton everything I know."

"Well, Miss Jeter," Tommy explained, "this isn't a police investigation. I represent a group of citizens here in town who want to make sure our city is governed and policed honestly and fairly for every resident, from the wealthiest to the poorest."

Wanda had a sort of glazed over look in her eyes after Tommy's first salvo. The councilman was afraid his speech was not only over her head but boring her as well. Tommy knew that there was no greater sin a man could commit than to bore a pretty woman. He chose to try and be more direct.

"Miss Jeter." He pitched his voice with as much sincerety as he could muster. "I, uh, all of us are very sorry for your loss. I know it must have been a great ordeal for you of late."

"Thank you." Wanda looked up him. "It has been a difficult time."

"And we," Tommy went on, "like you, wish with all our hearts that whoever committed this heinous crime will be brought to swift justice. We must trust our police to accomplish that. But many times these cases are like a rock dropped into a pond—there are ripples that spread beyond the base crime. Perhaps these ripples will reveal something or someone else that eludes detection by our local law enforcement."

He saw that glazed over look in Wanda's eyes again and he realized he had not really spoken any more clearly or directly at all. His academic, nearly purple prose, was lost on this woman. He had to try another approach.

Tommy redirected himself. "To be blunt, Miss Jeter, can you tell us who Mr. Cooper might have been involved with outside his world of baseball? Any doubtful characters perhaps?"

"Why heavens no!" Scandalized, she looked away. "I never spoke to Robert about any such thing."

"Well, Miss Jeter, it was apparently no great secret that Mr. Cooper had a lot of debts around town."

She continued to refuse eye contact. "I wouldn't know about that."

"Mr. Cooper didn't make a large amount of money playing ball, did he?"

Wanda shrugged, perhaps a little petulantly.

"Yet, he was always generous with you, was he not?" He raised his eyebrows. "He bought you nice things?"

A nod.

"Did he ever suggest how he got the money for these nice things?"

She made as if to speak, then seemed to think better of it.

"Other than using credit, of course."

Wanda merely shook her head again.

"What about names of people he might have mentioned?" Tommy went on patiently. "People you might not have been familiar with?"

"Like who?" She didn't look very pleased with any of his questions.

"Like Wade Smith?"

Wanda wasn't used to men grilling her like this. It confused and even annoyed her. She shook her head. She knew who Wade Smith was and she steered very clear of him.

"Henry Cottey?"

Her gaze turned serious. This was becoming more than she was willing to deal with. "Isn't he a Negro? Why would I know a Negro man?"

"No reason, ma'am." Tommy smiled politely. "How about Martin Patton? Did your Ace ever mention him?"

"No."

"All right, Miss Jeter." He sighed. He could see that he was not going to get anywhere with the attractive but uninvolved—or uninterested?—young woman.

"Perhaps it's too soon for you to be able to think about these things. Maybe you'll recall more as your grief eases. I'm sure you have many good memories of Mr. Cooper. Times that you shared and that will be with you always."

"Uh-huh."

She smiled demurely and smoothed a wrinkle in her dress. In that moment, Wanda recollected one of her last times with the redoubtable Ace Cooper. A shopping trip they had made to Cardwell-Ball, Jefferson's finest clothing store, right there on the west side of the city's busy town square.

SHOPPING AT CARDWELL-BALL'S

One Monday morning, a day when the Jefferson Redbirds weren't scheduled to play baseball, Wanda and Ace Cooper went up to the town square to shop for clothes at Cardwell-Ball's. The store's showcase windows were filled with mannequins dressed in the latest—mostly ladies'—fashions but some men's clothes were on display as well.

As the couple stood outside the store, Ace trying to act like he wasn't bored, Wanda noticed a pretty red dress on a mannequin in the window. Excitedly, she pointed at it. Ace checked out the only thing that mattered to him: the price tag. It read $18. Wanda grabbed Ace by the hand and pulled the handsome slugger into the store.

"Good morning." A well-dressed, matronly saleswoman walked up to greet the young shoppers. Wanda was already checking out a rack of expensive dresses when the lady came over to the couple. "Is there anything I can help you folks with?"

Wanda appraised the saleslady coolly. "Why, yes. Thank you."

Most of the sales people in town knew Wanda Jeter, knew her love of new things, knew she couldn't afford much of it on her own. This lady had waited on Wanda before, with previous beaus, and had learned to size them up, too.

This young man was tall and muscular, good-looking in a more citified way than most of the young men in the area. The saleslady correctly identified Ace as an out-of-towner. Another of Miss Wanda Jeter's conquests.

"There's a beautiful red dress in the window," Wanda told the woman, "do you have it in my size?"

The lady looked the young woman over with a keen eye. She knew that whatever size she suggested, the girl would want it in the next smaller one. Wanda Jeter's dresses always fit her a good deal too snugly as far as the saleslady and most of the other women in town who knew Wanda were concerned. Men on the other hand—well, they thought Wanda's clothes fit just right.

"I believe we do," the saleslady said. "Just over here, please."

"Oh, yes, there it is." Wanda was delighted when the garment in question was discovered on a rack just an aisle or two over. "I've just got to try it on. You don't mind, do you, Ace, honey?"

"Naw." Ace hemmed and hawed, shifting his feet back and forth. For a city boy, he never could understand why Wanda made him feel like such a country bumpkin.

"You're such a darlin', Ace." Wanda headed off with the saleslady towards a dressing room at the back of the store. Ace stayed where he was, whistling a tune and trying not to look like a complete idiot in front of the other sales people and customers in the store.

After what to Ace seemed like an inordinately long time to try something on, Wanda finally emerged from the dressing room wearing the brand new red dress. She sashayed back over to Ace and twirled around in front of him—and everyone else in the store, most of whom had actually stopped their own shopping to watch Wanda. The experienced saleslady came over with a string of imitation pearls and put them around Wanda's neck. Ace craned his neck to check the price tag. He thought it read $8.

Wanda pushed out a hip to show the lines of her body in the dress and fingered the faux pearls around her neck. "Do you like it, Ace, honey?"

Ace felt as if he might be sweating a little, and he was in a cool clothing store and it was still morning. For just this moment, he wished he were out at the fairgrounds ballpark, out in the field or up at the plate, somewhere where he was more comfortable, a place that he understood, with the guys, playing ball.

She pushed out her lips in a trademark pout. "Do you, Ace?"

"Uh, yeah. I guess. If you do."

"It's not too much is it, baby?" Wanda gave Ace her small-town girl look.

Ace grimaced. He knew darn well it was too much, but he would never say so to Wanda. If he didn't buy Wanda nice things, some other joker would and then he would be just like the other hicks and dumbheads on the team and in this little one-horse town—without a fabulous looking girlfriend. Ace had always had the best looking woman around. He took pride in it. It's just that this one, in this crappy little burgh, was costing him the most of all.

"No, baby," he lied with a smile, "it's not too much."

From out of nowhere, the saleslady produced a pair of shoes to complete the outfit.

"And these shoes, ma'am." She glanced over at Ace. "Would go perfectly with your dress and pearls. They're just ten dollars."

Ace suddenly felt like he might toss up the lousy bacon and eggs he'd eaten that morning over at the Cardinal Café just off the square. He longed for that simpler time he had imagined. He tried doing all the math in his head. It hurt him to do so.

The saleslady picked up Ace's vague reluctance. "I'll let y'all discuss it for a moment. Call me when you're ready."

"Thank you, hon." When the saleslady was gone, Wanda turned on Ace. "Is it just too expensive, Ace baby? I know they don't pay you much on that old team and all."

No shit, he said to himself.

"What is it altogether?" he asked out loud.

"I don't know, sugar, you checked all the tags."

Ace reddened. He had tried to be discreet about his tag reading.

"Let's see." He counted up the total silently, but his lips moved as he did so. "It's thirty-six dollars altogether. I think."

Wanda's eyes widened in concern. "Oh, Ace. That's more than you make all month playing ball, isn't it? I'll put it back. Even if it is so pretty. It does look nice on me though, doesn't it, Robert?"

Wanda always called him Robert when the chips were down. She knew he was a goner when she used his given name. Ace checked her out in the dress. She sure as hell did look good.

"Yes, yes." He nodded jerkily. "It's all right. You like it. I can put it on credit."

"Oh, Robert, sweetie," she cooed in his ear, "you're so good to me. But, baby, how will you pay for it?"

"Never mind about that, darlin'," Ace said, squaring his wide shoulders. "I can always come up with the money some way. You know old Ace. I never let you down, now do I? I always get the money."

"You always do, baby." She sidled up next to her generous man. "I don't know how, but you always do. You're just so wonderful."

He felt her warm body against his. His smile was a half-hearted and not very successful at hiding his discomfort.

Swallowing dryly, Ace signaled to the saleslady.

"We'll take these things," he called over to the woman, drawing air deep into his lungs.

She waved. "I'll be right there with the ticket. Y'all don't go nowhere."

Ace rolled his eyes and hoped nobody noticed. "Oh, don't worry. We're not."

COMING BACK TO TOMMY BALL

"Mr. Ball!" Mary popped into the councilman's doorway, her voice jarring Miss Wanda Jeter back into the present. "Pardon me, please. You asked me to remind you of the meeting. It's time to see the mayor."

"Of course, Mary. Thank you." He turned back to Wanda. "Miss Jeter, I'm afraid I have a meeting with the mayor that I must attend."

"Oh." Wanda was surprised. She didn't feel like much of anything had been said or accomplished during this so-called interview.

"But I do thank you for coming in." Tommy saw the furrow of doubt in her forehead and hurried to reassure the young woman. "We very much appreciate the help of concerned citizens like yourself in our effort to provide Jefferson with the best and cleanest government we can."

She really wasn't listening, though. "Yes."

Tommy didn't know whether the woman understood what he was saying— it sounded so much like one of his speeches before the Clean Government League that he wasn't sure it hadn't simply sailed right over her. Nevertheless, he did have to see the mayor and with no further ado, he rose and offered his hand to Wanda, which she shook.

"If you can think of anything at all about Mr. Cooper that might help us,

Miss Jeter, please feel free to contact me at any time. Thank you so much for taking the time to come by."

"All right," Wanda said softly.

"Good day, Miss Jeter."

"Good day, Mr. Ball."

Wanda stood up and without expression slowly walked out of the room. Tommy Ball and Mary Evans watched the swishing of Wanda's dress as the bereaved woman sashéd out into the hallway.

"Concerned citizen, my foot!" Mary said when Wanda was gone. "She no more cares. . . ."

Tommy gave Mary a sharp look that caused her to hold her tongue. She shook her head and frowned. Then with a sniff for her boss, the secretary marched out of the office and back to her desk. He shrugged his shoulders and hurried off to see the mayor.

CARL IN THE HOLLER

Carl Tatum had just gotten off work at the Ozark Hotel and was walking home past the Ozark County courthouse. As the tallest building in Jefferson, the courthouse—with its imposing spire towers and its dignified edifice of granite rock from local quarries along the White River—inspired awe in the citizens of the city and county, particularly among those who had felt the weight of the life-altering decisions rendered within its hallowed walls.

He reached the courthouse, jogged to the left a few feet and then made a right turn down the first hill that dropped quickly into the steep hollow where most of Jefferson's impoverished black population lived. This was Tin Hollow. Where the black citizens of Jefferson had survived together since the hopeful but ultimately failed days of the great Reconstruction.

As he traversed the dusty streets—some poorly paved with cracking asphalt or concrete, most still plain rocky Arkansas dirt—he passed many of the little homes typical of the hollow. Most of the little shotgun shacks were not much more than scrap wood and pieces of corrugated tin held together with bailing wire, including Carl's own home where his mother and father still lived today at the bottom of that first hill down into the hollow.

Carl still had a roped and blanketed off part of that old house that he had re-occupied after his days at Howard; but he spent little time there these days, preferring to work long hours at the hotel or rummaging through the local library, which surprisingly seemed to have no trouble allowing him in, or up at the university law shelves keeping up to date on the latest legal news. He drew stares in both places, but no one seemed to be concerned with his presence among books. Carl took advantage of the break in local custom to pursue the academic side of his long time goal: to become a real lawyer, right there in Jefferson.

Today, however, Carl was neither going home nor to one of the libraries. He had a different agenda. As he wound his way through the couple of fringe streets and alleys where Ola Mae's juke joint was and where the white ballplayer had been found and then on down and up the smaller hills of the hollow, folks occasionally nodding or speaking to him, Carl took in the sights of the neighborhood where he had been born and raised and which covered several small blocks on the east side of Jefferson.

Just past his folks' place at the bottom of the first hill in the hollow and up the next small hilly street, facing the back of the courthouse and the square beyond, was the "colored" school where local kids could get an education at least through the eighth grade. After that it was either move to Fort Smith or some other town that had a Negro high school, get a teacher who would train you themselves, try to eke out a living in the depressed local economy, or move to a larger city altogether, one where blacks had at least some possibility of finding work.

Half a block from the school, where he had been such an academic star among his peers—exciting hostility among some of the other boys and affection among several girls—Carl came upon one of the hollow's better homes. It belonged to Henry Cottey, the town's most successful, and of late its only, black moonshiner.

Cottey was a harsh, violent man and most people of Jefferson, black and white, gave him a wide berth. Rumor—more truth than speculation—had it that during the early years of prohibition, Cottey had removed his black moonshiner competition in a most vicious and permanent way. Carl and everyone in town knew that rumor and they gave the aggressive man his space.

Carl kept to the other side of the street as he passed by Henry Cottey's little whitewashed house with its cluttered front porch and weed-filled yard.

Just as Carl was across from the Cottey home, Henry's daughter Vera slinked out onto the front porch. Vera Cottey was as pretty and sweet as her father was ugly and mean. Wearing a dark, form-fitting, soft cotton dress that accentuated her earthy sexuality and full hips and breasts, Vera sauntered up to the rail on the front porch and leaned against it seductively. Carl tried not to look over but he couldn't help himself. Vera was just too pretty.

Before he had gone off to Howard, Vera had once made it very clear to Carl that her delights were available to him. She had pressed her warm, sumptuous body against him and kissed him in a way no other girl ever had. For reasons he still didn't fully understand he had found a way to resist her back then—maybe it was that she was too available, he just didn't know. But today he could not overcome the urge to at least look at her. When he did raise his glance to the porch, she winked at him.

"Hi, Carl Tatum!"

Carl let out a big breath of air. "How are you, Miss Vera?"

"Ain't seen you 'round lately." Carl stopped in front of the Cottey home and looked up at Vera. "Don't you be likin' me no more?" the girl asked.

"I figure you got enough beaus comin' round, you wouldn't need another."

Her smile was a mile wide. "We used to have fun 'fore you went off to that Coward College."

"Howard," he corrected. "Howard University."

"Whatever you say."

There was a brief lull and Carl made as if to go on, but Vera jutted one hip out and put a hand on the other hip in a very sexy pose clearly intended to stop him. It did. The young daughter of Jefferson's most notorious moonshiner smiled provocatively at the almost as young would-be lawyer.

"You know you always was my favorite."

"Uh-huh." He seriously doubted *that*.

"Where you off to in such an all-fired hurry?" Vera seemed offended. "Where you goin'?"

"I have to go see Mr. Carter."

"That old horseman?" She rolled her eyes and popped her fingers. "What you want with that stinky old man? He smell like them horses he keeps down in the pasture by them poor white folks."

"Mr. Carter is a fine man." Carl gave a little laugh. Vera's manner of speaking was as wild and appealing as she was herself.

She must have thought he didn't get it. "He's a stinky man."

Carl started to defend his friend Otis Carter again, but before he could get another word out a man's face suddenly appeared in a front window of the Cottey house. Carl recognized the face. It was Henry Cottey, Vera's father— sullen shoeshine man at a local white barbershop, incongruously a musician with a five-piece dance band playing mostly for white folks who always tried to pay him too little, the main moonshiner for Jefferson's black folks, and a handy man with a razor or a knife. It was general knowledge that he had killed at least two men and done prison time down at a state prison farm for one of them.

"You get back in the house, girl," the old moonshiner hollered gruffly out the window at Vera. "Right now."

"I'm just talkin' to Carl Tatum, daddy."

"I don't give a damn if you talkin' to Franklin Roosevelt," Cottey bellowed, "get back in here."

"Oh, daddy." She raised her eyebrows at Carl. He shrugged to show his commiseration.

"Good day to you, Mr. Cottey," Carl called up from the street.

Cottey grunted and disappeared from the window. Vera turned away walked towards the door of her house.

She looked over her shoulder and threw him another wink. "Bye, Carl. Maybe I see you later."

"Good day, Miss Vera."

"Vera!" old man Cottey yelled from somewhere inside the house.

Vera gave Carl a one last little wave and then hurried back into the house with an appealing little wiggle. Carl released a deep breath of air, turned to his left and hurried on to Otis Carter's house.

ROY HOLMES VISITS JEFFERSON AUTO REPAIR

Jefferson Auto Repair was located on Highway 71 right at the southern edge of town where the road meandered on its twisty path to, up, and through the Boston Mountains on the way to Alma, Van Buren, and Fort Smith. The dirty, loud, dual-bay shop was owned and operated by Wade Smith, an ex-con who had done hard time at the Arkansas State Penitentiary for car theft and extortion. Smith was originally from Jefferson and when he returned home he naturally gravitated towards local crime. That, naturally, brought him back in contact with two of his old Jefferson chums, the Patton brothers, Ned and Martin.

The relationship between Smith and Chief Ned Patton, in particular, was symbiotic, though officially nonexistent. It was rumored strongly that Smith fixed up stolen vehicles in his shop and turned them around for a profit, which he and his "friend" in local law enforcement split in, it was again said, 60-40 fashion. Smith getting the lesser of the two figures as befit his role as a glorified mechanic with a tight mouth.

Smith had other connections as well. Because of their frequent trips up and down Highway 71 from Louisiana and Texas to the south and Missouri and Illinois to the North, it was again rumored strongly that various members of the Barrow Gang, including Clyde and Bonnie herself, were no strangers to Mr. Wade Smith.

No one ever said anything of the sort out loud and it was never officially put in print by any overzealous local newspaperman, but circumstantial evidence seemed to point to some sort of connection between Wade Smith, Jefferson's power structure, and the infamous car-stealing, bank robbing gang.

On this fine summer day in 1935, just over a year since the famous outlaw pair had met their fate and with the sun burning away the residual coolness of the early morning to replace it with the steam heat normal for that time of year in the Ozarks, Wade Smith and his two shop hands, Mack Dyer and R. J. Jones, were hard at work detailing a black four-door Ford sedan. Smith and his boys were busy shaving some identification numbers off the block of the V-8 engine when Jefferson Patrolman Roy Holmes pulled up in his police cruiser and parked it next to the mostly broken up concrete curb alongside the road in front of the repair shop.

R .J. nudged Mack when he noticed Holmes arrive and Mack gave a similar nudge to Smith. Smith looked up with a harsh frown but Mack ignored his boss's standard hostility and just nodded towards the street. Smith looked over at the road and shook his head.

"You boys keep at it." Smith stepped away from the Ford and wiping the grease from his hands onto a greasy rag. "I'll go see what this dumb-ass wants."

"All right, boss." Mack and R. J. snickered at the approaching figure of Holmes but then went back to their work.

"Officer Holmes," Smith sarcastically greeted the patrolman at the front of the garage. "To what do we owe this pleasure? No parking tickets from the square, I hope."

"Naw." Holmes was always a little intimidated and uncomfortable with the gruff and often fear-inducing mechanic. "Just down on this end of town and thought I'd drop by for a second. Maybe get me a Coca-Cola."

Smith jerked a thumb over his shoulder. "You know how to get 'em out of the box. Five cents."

Holmes dropped a nickel on the counter and walked into the slightly cooler air of the shop's small, cluttered office, located the ice-box sitting on the floor to one side of the cash register and withdrew a chilled bottle of pop. He opened the bottle with a church key he found on the counter by the register, behind which was nailed a girlie calendar, and took a long satisfying drink.

Smith watched the policeman drink the soda with a look of complete disdain. Smith had no use for Holmes, or any police officer for that matter, even Chief Patton. Smith had had lots of experience with authority and it had left him permanently hostile, nearly violently so. Although he kept this attitude mostly in check in front of Ned Patton, he only did so because of their "business" relationship. With Holmes, on the other hand, Smith's attitude verged on the explosive at all times. His lack of respect for the patrolman was virtually palpable and tended, naturally, to be rather unsettling to Holmes.

After a few more drinks of soda, Holmes popped a piece of chewing gum into his mouth and, jawing it raucously, made the mistake of sidling up next to the taller, more muscular, and definitely rougher Smith. Smith instinctively drew back from Holmes, resisting an urge to hit the officer squarely between the eyes. Holmes, sensing Smith's hostility and noting the series of scars on the bigger man's face and neck—rumored to have come from a near death jailhouse knife fight—moved back a step himself.

When Holmes finally got up the gumption to speak, his tone was low, loud enough for Smith to hear but not enough so that he would be fully heard or understood by the young mechanics out in the bays whose work was occasionally punctuated by their own banter and by the intermittent sound of tools banging on metal and engines being revved and checked.

"I can't believe it." He cast a wary eye on Mack and R. J. to make sure they weren't tying to listen in. "He's let that smartass coon, Carl Tatum, go off tryin' to find whoever killed that ballplayer fellow."

"Who's he?" Smith knew the answer, but wanted to lure Holmes into backbiting Chief Patton. Always good to have a little dirt on people.

Holmes smacked his gum and took another quick slug of soda. "Hey, you know the chief."

"Naw." The big mechanic couldn't resist a sardonic smile for the policeman. "Which one was that that got killed?"

"His name was Robert—er, Ace Cooper. You didn't know him?"

Smith grunted. "Why would I know some such as him? I hear he got his ass killed over in the holler. Maybe that's why old Patton got that nigger boy, to see who done it."

Holmes was unimpressed. "I could'a done it just as well as him."

"You?"

"Why not?"

"You?" Smith laughed. "You talk to them colored folks about one of their own? You bein' pretty funny now."

"You're a good one to talk." Holmes decided to push his luck a bit. "You can't sell your shine to nobody in the holler, not as long as Henry Cottey's there."

Smith looked around for prying eyes and ears outside the garage, unconcerned about his own boys there in the shop whereas for Holmes it was just the opposite—he felt, since Smith so obviously had no respect for him that at least he had to seem authoritative to the two young mechanics. The boys acted like they didn't even know anything was going on beyond their auto work.

As for Smith, however, although he generally tolerated Holmes and his self-serving ramblings, references to Smith's moonshine business in a county still dry several years after prohibition had been lifted pretty much annoyed the auto repairman. He moved up very close to Holmes to address the patrolman.

"You'd be better off not talkin' about things you ain't got no idea about, boy," Smith said it almost directly into Holmes's ear. The officer's eyes darted wildly around the repair shop.

"I'm sorry, Wade." He moved back a step. "I didn't mean nothin'."

"Whoever this Cooper was—" Smith ignored Holmes's discomfort and edging the last step closer to the policeman, "—and I ain't sayin' I ever even heard of him—maybe he was doin' somethin' or bein' somewhere he wasn't supposed to. Maybe it was somethin' you be better off lettin' that black boy do the findin' out for you."

Holmes's voice was a little shaky. "M...Maybe it could be somethin' nobody would want to find out?"

"Maybe it would," Smith snarled. He hated whiners.

"But that boy will get all the credit if he finds out."

"Or get all dead."

Holmes looked away, took a drink of pop to hide his nervousness.

"Given where you work, you oughta know all that."

"Oh, yeah. Yeah, I know that." The patrolman tried to act as if he actually *did* know the inside workings of Jefferson's power structure—both legal and otherwise... which he clearly didn't.

Another grunt from Smith. "Uh-huh."

Holmes set his pop bottle on a windowsill and hitched up his uniform pants. He had had all of the repair shop he could stand for one day. "Reckon I better get on back to patrollin'."

"Yeah." Smith snorted. "You better do that. Old Patton's liable to replace you with that jig boy."

The rough mechanic had a good belly laugh at his own joke. Holmes would have liked to do something about Smith's sarcastic attitude but the mechanic was just too big and too tough. Instead, the patrolman just smiled and walked away, out to the patrol car. Smith watched the officer get in, start the vehicle, and pull off.

When Holmes drove away, Smith turned toward the garage bays and whistled loudly. Mack, the burlier of the two boys, who wore a gray shirt with his name sewed on the left pocket, looked up.

Smith signaled to him and the boy strolled up front to talk to his boss.

Mack was the first to speak. "Yeah?"

"You know a black boy named Carl Tatum?"

The mechanic nodded. "I know him."

"I give you the word, you pay him a visit, hear?"

"I hear."

"Now get on back to work."

"Yes, sir."

Smith turned away and Mack went back into the garage bays.

Smith stepped outside, took a pack of cigarettes out of his pocket and lit one up. With a rough smile, he blew smoke out of the corner of his mouth, watching it slowly curl up into the bright, hazy blue sky.

OTIS CARTER'S PASTURE

Otis Carter climbed through the barbed wire fence separating his modest but clean and well-kept home and yard—located at the end of a mostly poor white neighborhood—from his five-acre pasture at the back and side of his residence. He held the wire up for Carl Tatum to climb under.

"Thank you, Mr. Carter, sir," Carl said when he was safely out from under the sharp barbed wire and into the grassy pasture.

"Don't want you to cut your head on that wire," Otis said with a smile. "Wouldn't look good if my visitors was to go home with bloody heads." The older man let out a natural, happy laugh. Carl smiled.

"No, sir."

Otis, a tall, muscular man of about fifty years, walked slowly ahead of Carl, the two men making their way towards a pair of horses that were munching on the good green grass of the pasture. Otis raised and trained horses and the two animals there in the pasture, a bay and a buckskin, were feeding tranquilly at one far end of the L-shaped lot.

Otis took a bag of tobacco out of one pocket of his overalls and rolled and lit a cigarette. He offered to do the same for Carl but the younger man declined politely. Carl's attitude towards Otis Carter was one of respect and admiration, as befit the grandson of slaves and a man who had made a success of his life despite growing up and living in the Jim Crow south at its peak.

Carl surveyed Otis's home, yard, and pasture with the sweep of his right arm. "You've done real well for yourself here, Mr. Carter."

"It's all to my grandpap." Otis grinned. "he held out for the forty acres and a mule the guv'ment promised him when he got freed. This is what's left."

"It's real nice."

The old man stopped to check out a patch of wild, green grapes growing on a thick vine along the side of the barbed wire fence marking his pasture. He squeezed one and showed it to Carl.

"Not quite yet," he judged.

"The green ones will set you free," Carl deadpanned.

Otis let out a hearty laugh. "That's right, young fellow."

For a moment or so the men continued their slow walk towards the horses in silence, but then Carl broke the short pause by broaching the subject he had come to talk to Otis about in the first place.

"Mr. Carter, I have to tell you, sir, I came here for more than just a visit."

"I 'spected as much," the older man said, smiling.

"Sir, there's been a murder up at the edge of the hollow."

"Uh-huh." Otis rubbed his stubbly chin. "Some white boy went and got hisself killt there I hear."

It was Carl's turn to smile. "Yes, sir. I imagined you might have heard."

"Hard not to hear 'bout somethin' like that."

"Well, sir, they've asked me to help find out who did it."

"Who they?"

"The police chief."

"Ned Patton."

A nod. "Uh-huh. Also Tommy Ball of that new Clean Government League."

Otis shook his head. "There's a lot of things there, son, even for an educated boy like yourself."

Carl agreed.

"Lots of ways for a man to get hisself in some deep water."

"That's true, Mr. Carter."

"Well, you a grown man. You know what to do or not."

"I'm not so clear on some of it though, sir. That's why I'm here."

"Well, son, you know how proud we all is of you for goin' back and gettin' your lawyer schoolin' and all. Real proud. Even if they won't let you work regular up in that police and law thing they got goin' uptown."

"Thank you, Mr. Carter. I keep tryin'."

"I know you do, son." Otis patted Carl on the shoulder. "You're old Jess Tatum's boy; you'll come out fine. You'll be all right. But now tell me, what's this about you and that killin'? Why would they ast you to get in on it?"

He shrugged. "Well, sir, I have some ideas about that, but I wanted to hear what you might think. You know as much about Jefferson as anyone in town—black or white."

"I know some things," Otis allowed, "but this smells a little fishy to me, son. For one thing, I heared they done decided it was a black man done it before they even looked for anybody else. So the thing is, if that so, what does Patton and that Tommy Ball stand to get with you doin' the findin' out which one it was for 'em? Iff'n it even was one of us, which nobody know for sure yet anyway."

"Seems like a fair question to ask."

The old man looked at him gravely. "You'll be walkin' a fine line on this, you understand that?"

Carl nodded again. "Yes, sir."

They stopped in their walk. One of the horses, the buckskin, sauntered across the field and up to Otis. The horseman produced a handful of small carrots from a pocket of his overalls.

"All right." Otis reached out to pet the buckskin, and began feeding him carrots as he ran through the ins and out of the civics of Jefferson. "Well since you ast me, this here is what I'm thinkin'. First thing is: you gotta be very, very careful dealin' with these white folks. Even if the best of 'em is on the up and up, if you do something good they'll take credit for it and when somebody goes down for this murder they'll be wantin' to make it be one of us, sure as shootin', whether we done it or not."

Carl was a little surprised that Otis might have already thought of such a thing. "Are you suggesting it could have been a white killing?"

Otis held up a hand. "I ain't suggestin' nothing of the sort. I'm just sayin' it's still their world and they intend to keep it that way. They'll put it on anybody, includin' you, if they think they can or have to."

"I have a hunch it wasn't a Negro did it."

"Hunches can get you in big trouble, son. Stick with whatever the truth is, no matter where it leads."

Carl's voice rose. "That's what I'm lookin' for."

"Good. So let's get to it. I reckon you know some of what I'll be tellin' you, but I'll run it by the best way I know how."

"Okay."

Otis looked thoughtfully out across the field. "First off, Ned Patton is the real man in Jefferson. Ain't no question about it and it don't matter about no Mayor Turnbull or no Tommy Ball and his Guv'ment League. Patton runs the show. Don't nothin' happen—from moonshine to stole cars to city contracts and labor—without chief don't got his thumb in the pie. And it goes out from him: his brother at the county offices there; other family he got supplyin' God knows what to the city; and that Wade Smith fellow, he the one what runs the shine for white folks around town. Of all that bunch the one you best watch for is him, Smith. You know he run that garage over by the highway. That boy done time in the state penitentiary and he mean and hateful clean through and through. Still, he do the chief's biddin'. You watch out for him."

Carl looked at him with wide eyes. "I will. Thank you, sir."

"There's a bit more yet," the old man went on. "You're a smart boy, Carl, you seen the world some. There are white boys like to come to places like Ola Mae's over in the holler. They like their shine and they like their girls—don't matter the color. I'd be lookin' for somethin' there maybe for starters." Carl nodded his understanding. "Which also means the one who run most of our moonshine."

"Henry Cottey."

Otis nodded. "Henry Cottey. And that gal of his and others like her that be hangin' 'round Ola Mae's so much."

Otis fed the buckskin a final carrot, then patted the horse one last time. Satisfied with the little snack and attention, it slowly walked off into the field.

"Mr. Carter, I truly thank you for your wisdom, sir."

The old man cocked his head and grinned lopsidedly. "I don't know about no wisdom, son, but you watch yourself now. I see you have your hopes up with this."

"I believe," Carl said with some enthusiasm, "if I can work this one out like that Harley Brown case I did for them last year, they'll just about have to help me get my application to the bar down in Little Rock. Mr. Ball has said as much to me before."

"Well, I reckon it don't hurt a man to have hope sometimes."

"No, sir." Carl stuck out his hand and Otis took it warmly. "I don't believe it does. We can always hope. Nobody can stop you from doing that."

OTIS CARTER

Otis Carter's grandparents had been slaves, toiling most of their lives in the sticky, insect-infested cotton fields of the Arkansas Delta. When the Great War ended and with it the near unendurable pain of slavery, Grandpa Carter had taken his wife and three children, two of whom had to be retrieved from a farm just over the state line in Mississippi where they had been sold and taken mid-war, and moved his small, newly free clan up to the less rabidly hostile environment of northwest Arkansas.

The region had been split during the war, with nearly as many union sympathizers as confederate, and northern victory came early in the conflict. As a result, there was a small window of opportunity for freed blacks to live there without open reprisal and it was far from the cotton fields of the delta and the whips of the vicious farm overseers.

In the heady first days after the war, when Reconstruction looked like it might truly provide freedom for the hopeful ex-slaves, Grandpa Carter had applied for and actually received the forty acres and a mule that the U.S. Government, following up plans made by the newly assassinated President Lincoln, had promised every free black family in the south.

The forty acres was just south of the hilly county seat of Jefferson and it turned out to be surprisingly good land. Black dirt soil, rocky and hard to plow, but fertile and productive. Over the years, Grandpa Carter fashioned a decent enough life for his family. He traded extra crops for meat and such and bought a mare in the early 1870s who ended up, thanks to a neighboring stallion, producing a number of offspring that allowed the old man to actually become something of a horseman there at bottom of the Ozark Mountain hilltop upon which Jefferson sat.

His boys, particularly the middle one, Andrew (named after Old Hickory himself), had a knack for horses and the little family gained a reputation for both their riding abilities and for the quality of the horses they began to breed. Andrew, and his little brother Otis, were particularly good with the animals and they sometimes rode in exhibitions at the white folks' rodeos.

Meanwhile, Jefferson began to grow, to expand down off the mountain to the south. White people started moving towards the Carter farm and before they knew it, the Carters were surrounded mostly by poor whites trying to scratch a living out of far less land than the Carters had. This, coupled with the growth of the black community farther back towards town in an area called Tin Hollow—which now included a small store or two, an eating establishment, a church, and a school for black children—created a low level of hostility and animosity among some of the whites toward blacks in general and the Carters in particular.

Grandpa and Grandma Carter both passed in the '80s and the farm and animals passed into the care of Andrew and Otis. During that time there was a terrible depression back east and although northwest Arkansas, being a perpetually depressed economy, did not feel it as bad as the cities of the nation did (a similar phenomenon occurring fifty years later, then, during the Great Depression), Andrew was forced to sell ten acres of their land to a white banker named Dunston Ball to keep the family afloat.

About this time two major events occurred in the lives of the Carters. Andrew married a fine young woman named Sarah, up from the Pine Bluff area, and younger brother Otis caught the consumption and after a painful battle succumbed to the disease. When Andrew and Sarah had their first baby they named him Otis, too, after his lost uncle.

The boy Otis was a strong child and he was quick to learn about horses. By the age of ten, he could outride most men in the area. By his teens he was an attraction throughout the region at rodeos, horse shows, and parades. And the young Otis grew strong and tall and proud. It hit him particularly hard when his daddy had to sell most of their original forty acres, to that same white banker, to again keep the family solvent. They were left with just their home and a five-acre L-shaped pasture out of Grandpa Carter's original forty acres.

Daddy Andrew took the loss hard, too, and he died not long after. Otis, now a young man, sought a way out of the family's incipient poverty and history provided him with one—the next Great War, this one overseas. When the conflict in Europe broke out, Otis learned that the U.S. was forming some all-black units and the youngster found a way to enlist in one.

Otis did not actually fight in the war but he served at the front as a litter bearer and ammunition supplier on the Western Front and he was wounded twice and nearly blown up more times than he could count. He saved every dime he made and with some mustering out pay returned to Jefferson where he invested his money in horses and fixing up the family home for his momma.

In the years that followed, Otis, by now a confirmed bachelor—though not one without his opportunities—bought a good mare and bred her and started a small herd, members of which he would sell off from time to time to make ends meet. And he resumed his riding in local shows. As a local hero, albeit one of the wrong color, Otis had some notoriety and his natural pride and size and strength allowed him to carve out a world for himself in the midst of the segregated world that he had always lived in and had come back to.

His momma passed away in the 1920s and Otis settled into a life of quiet, solid work. The years went by and because of his steady success he became an unspoken leader of Jefferson's black community and a respected member of its entire society at large. People knew that Otis Carter was a full square man. Honest, dependable, good-natured, yet not the kind of man to be taken advantage of, by white or black.

He was often sought out for advice on horse rearing and training and he helped his neighbors with the plowing of their small fields and gardens. He still rode at the occasional rodeo or show and all in all was a good, solid citizen in this normally sleepy little town. He was the kind of man folks could trust and look up to. A strong man in the fullness of his years.

THE CHIEF CHATS WITH HENRY COTTEY

Police Chief Ned Patton had driven east to an old dirt road near the Green River bridge leading over to bordering Madison County. The chief parked his patrol car south of the bridge, an old rock and concrete affair that had looked obsolete the same day it had been erected more than two decades before.

It was another hot summer day and the chief fanned himself with a police report and sipped from a rapidly warming bottle of Coca-Cola to keep himself as cool as he could. Flies buzzed around the outside of the car, sometimes inside, and in a nearby field the chief could hear the lowing of some milk cows beginning to feel the need for their early evening milking.

In a few minutes, the chief heard another sound coming down the deserted country road—the rattling of a vehicle approaching from the other side of the bridge. The chief's car was in a dip in the road and could not be seen from the bridge nor could the chief see the oncoming traffic. But the lawman recognized the sound of a familiar old rattletrap truck heading his way.

And sure enough, just a moment later he could see the top of a black Ford pickup appear at the far side of the bridge. The truck slowly lumbered and banged along as more and more of it appeared above the rocky dirt road into the chief's line of sight. The truck crossed the bridge, slowed up for a moment as if the driver were considering stopping or turning back around, but then finally came on, stopping at last alongside the police car. Chief Patton looked over at the truck driver and nodded.

The driver nodded back.

"Henry Cottey," the chief said, as if announcing the main speaker at this year's upcoming policeman's conference.

"Chief Patton," Henry Cottey replied, in as noncommittal a tone as he knew how to muster.

"That's a fine pickup you got there, Henry." Patton smiled. "New side boards. Plenty of bed to haul, now, what you haulin', Henry? That ain't shine back there in them barrels, is it?"

"What you mean?" The chief had to be up to something. Everybody in a three county radius knew what Henry Cottey did, carried, and distributed. It wasn't no sarsaparilla.

Patton was no longer smiling. "I mean, is that illegal moonshine you're haulin' back there?"

Cottey looked confused, even a little worried now. "You knows plain enough what I do, chief."

Chief Patton laughed. Cottey stared at him in disbelief.

"Take it easy, Henry, I was just funnin' you." The chief slapped him on the arm, pleased with his little joke. "Just wanted to see you sweat some. That's all."

"Lord, that ain't funny, chief. You scare me half out of my wits. It's hot enough out here to make me sweat plenty, you don't need to help it none."

"All right, Henry," Chief Patton relented, "all right. No more funnin'."

"Yes, sir."

Patton finally decided to divulge his true motive for the encounter. "I come to see ya, knowin's how you usually out about here this time of week to see if you have your usual, uh, fee?"

The moonshiner scratched his head. "Fee?"

"Your usual fee."

"Oh, I gots it." Cottey finally caught the drift. He reached into a pocket of his overalls and brought out some bills. He passed them over to the chief, who carefully counted them out.

"Well, now, Henry boy," Patton said, done with his math, "this 'pears to be a might light. By weight I'd say about thirty dollars."

"I had me some extra, uh, costs," Cottey explained. "Unexpected like."

"Unexpected like." The chief smiled grimly. "Oh, we all get surprises sometimes."

"I pay you the rest here a week."

"Of *course* you will."

"You know I always does."

"But we been here before, Henry. You know this just can't be. How would it look if I didn't collect the city's fees for all this hauling around?"

"It's all I can afford this time, Mr. Chief. I swear. It's all I has to give."

The chief gave Cottey a long, hard look.

Cottey's eyes widened in fear. He'd known Ned Patton a long time. He knew the chief always had some way of collecting his "fees." Unable to wait for the chief to form a response, he pushed on. "Now what you thinkin'?"

Patton glanced around the countryside before turning his gaze back to the moonshiner. "I'm thinking that money ain't all a man like you might have that's worth somethin', Henry. Maybe you got somethin' not so unfeelin' as cash money."

Cottey pondered the chief's vague words. Their import finally settled in on him and the old moonshiner shuffled uncomfortably in his truck seat.

"I ain't got no such hold on that gal," he told the chief, "iff'n I get your meanin'."

The predatory smile returned. "Sure you do."

"I cain't tell her to do no such thing. She's strong willful, Mr. Chief. Like her momma was."

"Oh," the chief said with a wink, "I do remember her momma."

"Then you knows what she like. I ain't got no pull on her."

Patton sniffed. "Since when? You and her turn over a new leaf? I thought when you barked that girl run."

"I don't know." The chief knew he'd won by the sound of resignation in Cottey's voice.

"You got that money then?"

"No, sir."

"Well."

"All right." Cottey gave in. "You come round when you want. I cain't guarantee nothin' though."

"Now that sounds better. I usually check the holler early in the mornings. Good time of day for that."

Cottey's gaze wouldn't meet Patton's "Yes, sir."

"Okay, then, Henry. We be seein' ya."

Chief Patton restarted the patrol car and with a wave to Cottey drove on down the road towards the one lane bridge. Cottey did not look at the chief, nor did he return the wave. He just stared straight ahead until the chief was well on away from him. Then he hit the gas and his truck lurched forward.

"White son of a bitch." He drove away, the truck rattling and clanging down the dusty back road. In the nearby fields, the milking cows kept up their lowing cries. Cottey drove on cursing to the empty sky and road.

CARL CHATS WITH A BALLPLAYER

Carl Tatum was tending bar in the seldom-used lounge of the Hotel Ozark one blessedly cool evening while Jack Rucker, the tall Jefferson Redbirds first baseman, sat at the counter drinking from a thin, gold flask. Rucker was already three sheets to the wind when he had staggered into the Ozark and the night manager gave Carl the task of waiting on and keeping an eye on the inebriated ballplayer.

Rucker, tiring of his warm alcohol, ordered a soda water with ice and watched like a mother hawk as Carl prepared the drink. When he finished and set the glass in front of the disheveled ballplayer, Rucker set his flask aside and pulled a pint bottle of moonshine from an inside pocket of his jacket. Silently he loaded up the soda water and ice with a generous amount of shine.

Carl reached below the counter, produced a silver tray of peanuts, and set the tray in front of the ballplayer. "Would you care for some peanuts, Mr. Rucker?"

Rucker took a handful, dropping a few on the counter. "Oops."

"That's all right, Mr. Rucker," Carl said casually as he retrieved the stray peanuts and set them on a napkin that he placed on the top shelf behind the bar. They would make a good snack later.

"Yeah, thanks," Rucker mumbled, looking up at Carl and reacting as if he were aware of him for the first time.

Carl began wiping down the counter with a rag. "I was awful sorry to hear about your friend, Mr. Cooper, sir. It was a real sad thing. A strong man like that cut down in the prime of his life."

"It wadn't fair."

The young man agreed. "It don't seem like it."

Rucker grumbled drunkenly. "What would you know? Ace was a great guy. A real buddy. How would you know?"

He shrugged, as if he didn't know what exactly to say. "It was a real sad thing. A strong man like that cut down in the prime of his life."

Rucker hammered back more of his moonshine and soda. He waited for the outburst to die down.

"It's hard to figure who would have killed a fine man like Mr. Ace," Carl pressed on after it seemed Rucker's annoyance had passed. "Or why."

"Ace just liked to have fun." The ballplayer's voice dropped even lower. "He liked the ladies."

Carl busied himself by drying an already dry glass. "Uh-huh."

"Oh, and that Wanda." Rucker whistled. "He would do anything for her."

"Anything?"

"Anything." A nod. "He bought her fine things and she didn't never 'preciate 'em."

"No."

"No," Rucker said, "and I told him, too. Sometimes he couldn't stand it and he would go to Ola Mae's. Find a nig—"

"Uh-*huh*."

Rucker went on. "But I told him. I warned him. Shoot, it wadn't hardly a week ago or so I was sayin' to Ace out on the field…."

RUCKER AND ACE AT THE BALLPARK

On a hot afternoon at the ballpark not long before Ace Cooper was killed, while the Redbirds warmed up before a game, Jack Rucker and Ace stood side by side in foul territory down the third base line near the browning outfield grass. Each of them played catch with another player standing back up the line closer to the dugout. Ace and Rucker chatted as they loosened up their throwing arms.

"Look at her over there, Ruck." Ace pointed excitedly.

Rucker glanced over at Wanda Jeter in the bleachers where she sat in back of the Redbirds dugout. Wanda, dressed in a colorful summer dress, a mix of blues and greens, looked her usual terrific self. She wore a large stylish hat, perfect for keeping the harsh sun off her nearly alabaster skin.

"I see her." Rucker hid a sigh. "I see her."

Ace marveled. "What a woman."

Rucker grunted. "Uh."

"I'd do anything to keep her, man. I ain't kiddin'."

"You already do."

"What's that supposed to mean?" Ace raised an eyebrow.

"Damn, Ace. You spend more money on that woman than the whole team makes."

"What of it?"

"What of it?" Rucker laughed. "Jeez, everybody knows what you're doin'. Fer Chrissakes, you're walkin' a fine line here, man."

This drew a snort. "So what?"

"You're messin' with people can get you hurt, buddy. These little towns down here, they don't like us outsiders comin' in here and messin' 'round."

"Nobody says nothin' to me," Ace countered.

Rucker poked him in the chest with a stiff index finger. "And you're hittin' it pretty hard over in Tin Hollow."

The other man stepped back. "Yeah? Well, what do you expect me to do? Never get none like the rest of you Sorry Charlies? I need me some poon ever now and then. Wanda is a lady; I have to go to the hollow for my fun."

Rucker threw up his hands in frustration. "Your fun can get a man busted up. This can be a rough little town in them back streets. It's hard to tell the moonshiners from the cops sometimes—maybe most of the time—and vice versa."

"I wouldn't know."

"Right." Rucker sniffed. "Like I don't know old Calvin over there ain't dyin' to take a slot in the lineup any time you foul up."

Ace laughed. "Don't worry about me. I know what I'm doin'."

"I'm just tellin' ya, that's all."

CARL AND RUCKER
BACK IN THE OZARK LOUNGE

Rucker, lost for several moments in his memory of himself and Ace at the ballpark, came out of his internal recollection talking and angry.

"I told him." The ballplayer addressed his glass of soda water, moonshine, and ice. "I told him to watch his step."

Carl wanted to keep the drunken man talking.

"I reckon you did your best to help him, Mr. Rucker."

"I tried," Rucker moaned. "I tried."

"Sure you did. You did all you could. You did your best for your friend."

"My friend—" Rucker began, then suddenly stopped.

He looked at Carl again as if he had never seen him before or known to whom he was talking—a colored waiter in a crappy little one-horse town hotel bar. Rucker's mood shifted rapidly, and his face turned bright red. "You just never mind about Ace. You don't understand nothin' of it. Butt out, boy."

"I was just trying—"

"Stay out of stuff ain't none of your business."

"Sorry, Mr. Rucker," Carl said sincerely, "I'm sorry."

"You're pokin' your black nose into things ain't none of your concern," Rucker said, his drunken face contorted into a nasty sneer.

Carl stiffened and took a step back. "Never mind that then. I apologize. Here, have another glass of soda water and ice—on the house."

"Yeah, yeah."

The young man quickly made up the other glass of soda water and fresh ice and set it before Rucker. It seemed to adequately mollify the baseball man and he began to calm down.

"Just don't unnerstan'," He seemed to have moved into an even more inebriated stage and the conversation ended with another set of barely coherent words. "None of your business. None."

"Yes, sir, Mr. Rucker." Carl realized he would get no more information from the ballplayer on this evening. "Yes, sir."

ONE AFTERNOON
BEHIND THE MAYOR'S CLOSED DOOR

At Mayor Alton Turnbull's request, five of Jefferson's heaviest political hitters, including the mayor himself, Police Chief Ned Patton, his brother and ally County Assessor Martin Patton, and the Patton's nemeses Councilman Tommy Ball and his fellow Clean Government Leaguer, local entrepreneur Richard Lee Hudson, had gathered together in the mayor's office for a closed door session.

The mayor had called the unscheduled session to "try and clear the air," as he had told the skeptical participants a couple of days before. Mayor Turnbull, not a particularly energetic public servant but one who understood the benefits of a tranquil populace, believed that the ongoing "difference of opinion" between the Patton forces and the Clean Government League was detrimental to the good of all specifically involved and of the Jefferson community in general.

He was well aware, he had told the conflicting parties, that there was a gulf in ideas between them—as the stream of lawsuits filed by the Clean Government League aimed at and designed to remove the police chief had made abundantly clear—but Mayor Turnbull felt the antagonists could find a way to settle their differences amicably, and in a mutually beneficial way.

"Gentlemen," the mayor began, using his role as the city's nominally highest ranking official, at least he had been elected as such, to open the discussion among the warring sides. "I want to get right to the point. I'm not pleased with the way things have been transpirin' here in Jefferson of late—not pleased at all."

The mayor looked around at the others to gauge their sentiments. Tommy Ball and Richard Lee Hudson seemed fine with his honor's opening statement, but the look of sheer disrespect, even hostility, on the faces of the police chief and his brother made the mayor look up at the ceiling of his office and let out a breath of air.

Ever supportive—and ingratiating—Tommy Ball gave a little bow. "We couldn't agree with you more, mayor."

"Amen." This from the pious Richard Lee.

Chief Patton shook his head in disgust. His brother Martin looked down at his shoes like they might be getting ready to jump up and bite him.

Chief Patton sneered at the Clean Leaguers. "Naturally you two would go along with that."

Tommy Ball responded with a sharp look, which the chief laughed off.

The mayor decided to intercede "Gentlemen, I have to tell you, I see both of you as part of the problem."

Lee looked scandalized. "Sir, that's patently not fair."

"Be quiet, Hudson." Martin Patton rolled his eyes. "You don't know what you're talking about. You never do."

Tommy Ball pointed at the Patton brothers. "That's the problem right there in a nutshell, Mister Mayor."

Martin snarled at Tommy, but the chief just responded with another laugh. He was apparently trying to act as if anything Tommy Ball and the Clean Government Leaguers said was purely laughable nonsense. It was the same tactic he'd used to good effect so far in the lawsuits brought against him by these interfering, mamby pamby, do-gooders.

Martin read the chief's thoughts. "Dumb do-gooders."

"Thieves," Lee spat back.

Chief Patton, with a mirthless smile, held his brother back, then signaled for the mayor to continue. Martin sat down but stared harshly at Lee. For his part, Lee did not look over at the pugnacious County Assessor.

Chief Patton decided to steer the conversation back to its original beginning, "Mister mayor, make your point, will you? I've got work to do."

"Tommy, Richard." The mayor waved a chubby arm around like a wand. "I have to tell you, your Clean Government League is giving Jefferson a black eye in the newspapers. It doesn't help our merchants if people who might want to invest in Jefferson, or who might just want to shop here, read all about us and believe that we are as corrupt as you fellows paint us out to be."

"But we *are* that corrupt," Ball said. "and the CGL intends to take Jefferson from the dirty hands of the corruptors and give it back to the people."

"For God's sake," Martin growled. "CGL—what's that, more of your Eleanor Roosevelt talk? CCC, WPA, CGL. Ever since you met that woman you can't talk with anything but initials. And give it back to the people—who are they, the coloreds? That's just more of your Roosevelt, socialist claptrap."

Ball's face began to redden. "I'll have you know, Patton, that Mrs. Roosevelt is one of the finest ladies who ever lived. She believes in a square deal for all Americans. Every last one. White or colored."

"Bullshit, you commie liar."

"That's *enough*, Martin," the mayor said. "You Patton boys have barely enough room to talk yourselves."

Chief Patton's eyebrows went up. "What's that supposed to mean, Turnbull?"

"It means, chief," the mayor said, more bravely than he felt, "that more charges are about to be brought against you."

Patton sniffed, waved it away. "Old news."

"New news, Chief Patton," Tommy Ball retorted. "Felony auto theft, distribution and acceptance of illegal monies from known criminals, consorting with known criminals, tax. . . ."

"Enough, Ball. I know the damned charges. I've beaten them before."

"Maybe you won't be so lucky this time. Maybe the chief witness won't suddenly decide to leave the state like the last time."

"He left of his own accord," the chief said.

Tommy laughed. "Right."

"You pissant," Martin Patton said coarsely.

"Stop it." The mayor slammed his hand down on the desktop. "Stop it right now. Regardless of what has happened or not, the charges against the chief certainly are of significance here, too. They hurt the city. If we're seen as some outlaw hillbilly town, we're just not going to be able to grow economically. And we've got to find our way out of this depression."

"Jefferson has never known any other way." Lee shook his head ruefully.

The mayor held out his hands, palm up. "It's time, then, to change that. And I'm asking all of you gentlemen here to help, to help Jefferson, to help yourselves, to help ourselves, to get us back on the up and up, on the road to a better tomorrow. Will you do that? Try to do that?"

The Patton brothers shuffled in their seats and mumbled unintelligible oaths under their breath. Hudson and Ball nodded their agreement.

"Good. That's at least settled. Now to a specifically pressing problem. Chief, where do we stand on that Cooper murder investigation?"

The Chief looked away. "We're on it."

Ball laughed. "You mean Carl Tatum is on it."

"Yes," the mayor said. "That's right. And I have to say that I don't quite get this one. Why is it again that a colored boy is working on this investigation?"

"Well, he's not really doing the investigation, mayor." Patton's patronizing tone grated on the mayor. "I just have him checking a couple of things for me with the colored folk down in the holler."

"What a load." Tommy Ball rolled his eyes. "Without Carl, Mr. Mayor, there wouldn't even be an investigation. As far as I can tell, there is precious little work being done by our police force."

Patton snorted. "As far as you can tell."

The mayor leaned back in his chair. "Well, what have we got on the murder—from this Tatum boy, or the police department?"

The chief was growing bored. "I take the crime to have been perpetrated by a nig —colored person. Probably an out-of-towner."

"For crying out loud." Lee spoke to his shoes, thereby not seeing the murderous looks he received from the Patton brothers.

"Mr. Mayor," Tommy Ball said, "I've talked to Carl recently and I believe he immediately debunked the chief's first colored suspect, Floyd Meadows."

"Floyd Meadows?"

Patton grasped his lapels proudly. "We eliminated old Floyd right away."

"You mean *Carl* did," Ball said.

"You know, Ball, you sure are keen on that boy, ain't you?" Hostility dripped from the chief's every word.

Ball's voice dripped equally with disdain. "That 'boy,' as you call him, has a law degree."

"It don't change his skin color none," Martin Patton said.

Lee cleared his throat. "It does make him more educated than any man in this room, though."

The mayor glanced up at the ceiling with a resigned expression. "Let's bring Tatum in, then. Talk to him. See what he's found."

Patton dropped his chin in frustration. "We're not likely to learn anything new from him, mayor."

Ball jumped on the admission. "Then why's he still on the case?"

"Never mind about that." The mayor asserted himself before the chief could ready a response. "Let's get him in. Soon as we can."

The Pattons grumbled over the prospect of Carl Tatum being brought in to the city's official business. Tommy Ball and Richard Lee Hudson exchanged smiles. The mayor settled back into his comfortable, soft leather mayor's chair.

"See to it, then," he said grandly to Chief Patton. "Bring that Tatum boy on in here."

OLA MAE'S RESTAURANT AND JUKE JOINT

Monday to Wednesday, Ola Mae's little restaurant and juke joint on the edge of Tin Hollow mostly catered to working men from the hollow who wanted a good, cheap meal and a beer or two. But late night Thursday through Saturday the place took on a different tone as Ola Mae had a local three-piece band, The Juke Boys, playing jump music on a piano, an old set of drums, and a big, worn looking upright bass. Local couples, married or otherwise and looking for a place to dance and unwind, would scrape enough money together for the weekend and along with the band they turned Ola Mae's into a hopping place.

Sometimes, as had so recently and fatally occurred, an occasional white boy—usually an out of towner, lately from the new professional baseball team in town or some such thing—or an even more occasional white couple out to experience the excitement, and maybe danger, of going to a mostly all black club, would show up and then things could get a touch out of hand.

Ola Mae did her best to keep the peace, but conflicts could flare up between the bar-crashing white boys and local young bloods—invariably over the attentions of one of the regular girls who came to Ola Mae's—Vera Cottey being one of the most sought after girls and the one over which most of the disturbances started.

On a sultry August Saturday night, with the recent death of Robert "Ace" Cooper still fresh in her mind, Ola Mae stood by the door of her kitchen keeping a watchful eye on the club. The last thing she needed was trouble with the local police, especially that greedy Chief Patton, coming around, nosing around, scaring away her cash-strapped customers, maybe making up one of his excuses for putting his fat white hand into her till.

The band was on Ola Mae's left as she stood with her back to the kitchen area and she smiled as she watched two thirty-ish couples dancing in the middle of the smoky room, swaying back and forth to a slowed up tune played by The Juke Boys. At a back table, another couple sat drinking and whispering quietly to one another. All looked well there. Behind her, in the kitchen, Dinty Blaine went about the business of making up some fried fish, greens, and potatoes for one of the hungry couples there in the club.

Back in a dark corner of the bar, however, Ola Mae could see two young bloods standing side by side, swilling strong drinks, and doing some heavy "interacting" with Vera Cottey. Ola Mae frowned as she watched Vera openly and physically show her receptivity to the attentions of the two men. *That girl,* Ola Mae thought, *bound to get some man killed, if she hadn't already.*

As the slow Juke Boys' tune wound down, the outside door to the joint opened and Carl Tatum entered. Ola Mae turned towards the door and watched Carl as he took a moment or so to adjust his eyes to the light in the club.

Carl nodded to Ola Mae. "Evenin', Miss Ola Mae."

"Evenin', Mr. Tatum." Ola Mae smiled at young Carl's formal tone. "How can we help you tonight?"

"I'm just looking to talk to Dinty, ma'am." Carl saw the old cook working back in the kitchen. He waved, but the old man acted like he didn't see.

"Well, he back there. Workin'."

"Yes, ma'am." With another polite nod, he started on back to see Dinty.

Across the room, Vera Cottey also noticed Carl's arrival. Immediately breaking off from her two suitors, she made a beeline toward the front of the bar, trying to cut off Carl's path to the kitchen.

As the girl approached, Ola Mae feinted as if to intercept her. Vera rushed past and stopped Carl a step from the kitchen door, thrusting her body in front of—practically against—him.

Carl pulled up abruptly. The Juke Boys ended their song and Vera spoke into the quiet of the room, Ola Mae hanging nearby, listening openly.

"Why, Carl Tatum." Vera moved her hips from side to side seductively. "What you doin' up in here? I didn't think you come 'round since you a lawyer boy and all now"

He took a step back. "I came to see Dinty Blaine."

Vera put her voluptous body firmly against Carl and moved up and back on him, side to side. He tried to disentangle himself from her and get by.

She gave a false little cry. "Don't you want to see me?"

He sighed. "Vera, I'm on business."

As Carl tried again to separate himself from the clinging girl, the two youngbloods who'd been working Vera came up alongside. Ola Mae, sensing trouble, moved into the doorway leading back to the small kitchen.

"What you wantin' with her?" This one wore a dirty fedora and a three-inch scar across his chin.

Carl detached himself from Vera. Slighted and petulant, she moved away crossing her arms over her chest.

The second snobby young Turk, a stocky, hard-eyed kid, stepped up. "She with us."

"Nobody with you," Vera sniffed.

Scar put a hand in his pants pocket and something flashed with a distinct metallic and silvery sheen. "Step back, friend."

Vera rolled her eyes. "Don't listen to these fools, Carl. They ain't got no claim on nobody or nothin'."

The stocky one put his hand on Vera's arm, but she slapped it away.

"You best be movin' on," Scar warned.

Carl raised his hands. He wanted no trouble, but the two young bloods moved menacingly towards him.

Suddenly Ola Mae stepped between them, Dinty Blaine appearing as if by magic from the kitchen to back her up. Dinty brandished a big, sharp meat cleaver. In Ola Mae's hand was a small .32 caliber revolver. She rested her thumb on the hammer, ready to cock the weapon. "That's enough of this nonsense right now. You two need to be movin' on. Right now."

"Easy there, woman."

Scar sneered. "Don't be pointin' that thing at me. I don't cotton to no threats from no old woman."

"I'll do more than point it at you," Ola Mae said with conviction. "Now git your trashy selves out of my club. There's none of this gonna happen here. I got enough trouble without the two of you stirrin' up anymore. Go on. Git. And watch who you callin' an old woman, boy."

The two toughs snorted and styled a bit but stayed where they were. Dinty raised his meat cleaver.

The stocky blood decided it was smarter to move on for the time being.

He slapped his buddy's shouder. "C'mon. Let's get out of this dive hole. We go find some real action someplace else."

Scar jerked his head at Carl. "I'll be seein' you around," he growled as the they headed slowly for the door.

Carl held his tongue.

"Git," Ola Mae spat. "Now you git on out, right this minute."

The pair walked casually out the door, slamming it behind them. In their wake, Ola Mae's joint stilled. Everyone in the place was watching her.

She lowered the pistol. "What is it that you want here so much, Carl? You come in here stirrin' up trouble and all."

Carl worried the bill of his hat. "Miss Ola Mae. I am truly sorry. I wasn't lookin' for trouble. Honest."

"I think trouble find a good man," Vera cooed, sidling up next to Carl again.

"It do if you around, girl," Ola Mae said. Vera, annoyed by the older woman's tone, looked away haughtily.

He cocked his head and smiled in embarrasment. "I was just wanting to talk to Dinty for a minute, that's all. I swear to you, Ola Mae."

"What you want with me?" Dinty's meat cleaver, now at his side, still gleamed brightly in the light of the overheads.

"Put that thing down, Dinty, before you cut yourself." Ola Mae turned back to Carl. "What you after? It ain't about that dead white boy again, is it?"

"Yes, ma'am." Carl nodded. "It is."

"I don't know nothin'," Dinty chimed in.

He tried to reassure the jumpy cook. "Just a couple of questions, Mr. Dinty. Nothing more."

"I done told that police man everthing."

Carl kept his voice even. "Miss Ola Mae—is there some place where Dinty and I can talk, private like?"

"If you think you have to, honey, you can use my office in back there." Ola Mae pointed beyond the tables where the few remaining people sat, waiting to see if there would be more fireworks. "But if I was you, I'd stay out of white folks' business."

"Yes, ma'am. Thank you very much, ma'am."

"I don't see why I gotta say the same danged things agin." Dinty growled.

"C'mon, Mr. Dinty." Carl smiled. "It won't take us five minutes. You'll see."

"I just don't see why." The old man dropped his meat cleaver noisily beside the kitchen grill.

Carl put his arm around Dinty's shoulder and led the old man to a small door in back of the café behind which was Ola Mae's tiny business office. When the two men were all the way at the back of the club, Ola Mae turned her attention back on Vera. She looked directly into the girl's eyes and was met by a corresponding steady glare.

After a couple of moments of their visual version of a Mexican standoff, Ola Mae finally spoke. "So what is it that you want?"

"Nothin' from you." Vera popped her head back and sniffed the air.

"Well, either settle yourself down or find your way on out of here for tonight," Ola Mae said. "You've done stirred up your usual brew already anyway."

Vera's expression was one of disgust. "Maybe I'll just leave and won't come back to your dirty old place."

"Fine by me. Won't hurt me none."

Vera grunted, but did not pursue the argument.

After another exchange of glares, Ola Mae turned away and headed back into the kitchen. Vera made a face at her departing figure. As if on cue, The Juke Boys struck the first notes of a new song and a pair of relieved couples got up to dance again. As the band kicked up the beat, Vera tossed her head back proudly and crossed the dance floor by herself. She swayed to and fro as if dancing with an invisible partner. From the kitchen window, Ola Mae looked out at her and shook her head.

"Don't know why I keep this blessed place open at all," she said to herself as she hacked a wing off a whole chicken with the meat cleaver Dinty had left behind. "Don't know why I do it at all."

BY THE POST OFFICE

Carl had dropped off some hotel letters up at the post office on the town square, taking a few moments to review the pictures of the Ten Most Wanted criminals in the U.S., and had just stepped back out onto the landing of the set of concrete stairs leading east from the building and down a few feet to the square itself. It was a beautiful day, if going to be a hot one, and Carl breathed in deep the clear air and admired the fully-leaved oak and maple trees around the post office grounds and the bright mix of flowers in several symmetrically spaced garden boxes.

Just as Carl began to descend the steps of the post office, still enjoying the beauty of the day, he was surprised to find himself suddenly face to face with Jefferson Chief of Police Ned Patton. The chief smiled at Carl real friendly like but made no effort to move out of Carl's way. Carl nodded a silent greeting and started to step around the chief. The chief calmly raised a hand. Carl stopped.

"Walk with me a bit, Carl," the chief said pleasantly, but firmly.

"All right, Chief," Carl said, understanding that the chief's words were an order not a request.

The chief put an arm around Carl's shoulder briefly and headed the two of them on down the steps. When they reached the street level of the square, the chief kept them at a slow amble as they traversed the four sides of the square while carrying on their conversation. All around them, the store owners and clerks and their customers went about business as usual, paying little heed to the chief and his companion. An occasional car rattled by as the men talked, and the chief seemed relaxed and comfortable—in a good mood. Carl, on the other hand, had found the sudden appearance of the chief rather unnerving and it made him a little tense, somewhat reticent and guarded in his speech.

"We were wonderin', Carl," the chief said mildly, "if you learned anything yet down there in the holler."

"I've picked up a few things."

"And?" Chief Patton held out an open palm as if to receive the younger man's words in them.

"And?"

"You mind sharin' 'em with me?" The older man's voice was not so mild now as before.

"Not at all, sir," Carl said, not wanting to annoy the chief intentionally.

"Well?" Patton sighed. His patience was beginning to wear thin.

"Well," Carl said, "you may not like where all this is going to end up."

"Let me be the judge of that," the chief smiled. It was a grim, humorless smile. It made Carl nearly wince and he looked away from the big lawman.

"It doesn't look like any Negro did the killing like you were, uh, expecting." He took a brief look at the chief's face. It betrayed no reaction he could discern other than interest.

"No?"

"No, sir," he went on. "Seems like Mr. Ace Cooper was something of a wild boy. Got in a little too deep with local moonshiners. White ones."

The chief snorted, trying not to laugh. "You don't say, now? And who could have told you such things. Ola Mae?"

"I have my sources." Carl said, a little more defensively than he had meant to.

"Dinty Blaine?"

Carl sidestepped. "He was selling shine to the upper class white folks."

"Do tell," the chief said in the standard ironic tone he adopted with those he considered his inferiors—which included practically everyone in town, and for certain all the blacks.

When Patton used that tone it made Carl wonder if the chief really did know all about the murder or if he was just another Jim Crow small town cop talking big. Why had the big policeman called Carl in? What were his motives? The attempt to pin this crime on poor Floyd Meadows had been so easy for him to knock the underpinnings off of that it was hard to figure out Patton's motives for keeping him around. What was this small-time town boss up to? He decided to throw caution out and tell some of what he knew.

"I was told about this party, Chief Patton." He smiled. "It happened sometime back."

RICHARD LEE HUDSON
HOSTS AN EVENING PARTY

Richard Lee Hudson, city reformer and social climber in Jefferson's elite inner circles, moved through the chatting, visiting crowd in his spacious living room. Hudson and his wife, Mary, were hosting a fundraiser that brought out a wide mix of local socialites, business people, and minor town celebrities. The Hudson's large Victorian house was located in the city's oldest and most prestigious section, a clean, well-kept part of town dotted with many homes similar to Hudson's, most of which were built during a brief period of growth in Jefferson that had occurred between 1900 and 1930.

Among the well-knowns at the party were: Mayor Turnbull, Tommy Ball, Richard Lee's compatriot in the Clean Government League, and other leading area entrepreneurs, including Pete Henry, owner of the local professional baseball team. Mr. Henry had drug along Fred Casey, the team's likable manager, but despite the informal hospitality of the occasion Fred couldn't have felt more out of his element had he been in an opposing team's dugout during the playoffs.

Walt Harrison, the short, rail-thin, and humorously cynical local news and sports reporter was there also, as well as a generous array of up and coming young men accompanied by their wives or girlfriends. Conspicuously absent from the soiree were any members of the Jefferson police force.

Conspicuously present, though currently unattended as Richard Lee passed by her at the edge of the living room, was Wanda Jeter. Wanda reclined on a large divan and while she was openly or surreptitiously ogled by most of the men—to the chagrin of their women—she kept an eye on the front door as if anticipating another arrival.

Among the people working the party and waiting on the bon vivants were several local blacks, including the ubiquitous Dinty Blaine, who appeared to have a knack, unwanted though it may have been, for being in places where the action was. Dinty moved through the crowd offering a punch drink, which was sniffed and usually accepted, though with what appeared to be a certain reluctance. Dinty could scarcely avoid overhearing snippets of talk as he went through the room.

"Why, yes, that's right," Mayor Turnbull was explaining to a small group gathered to hear the utterances of hizzoner. "All three girls are to be married on the same day. We are so proud of. . . ."

Just beyond the mayor was Tommy Ball, expounding on his favorite topics, the Roosevelts and the New Deal.

". . . an equal chance for everybody." Tommy moved slightly to let Dinty Blaine get past with his tray of drinks. "That's the promise of the New Deal. Why, I just read that President and Mrs. Roosevelt . . . ."

Beyond Tommy were the sports people.

Walt Harris gave Pete Henry a needling grin. "Tell me Pete—are the boys going to win it all for you this year?"

"You bet they are, Walt," Pete shot back in his optimism-at-all-costs manner, "but not just for me, no, sir. For all of Jefferson. They're a swell bunch of boys."

"That is," Walt kept up his teasing banter, "if old Fred here can just keep 'em in line, huh, Fred?"

"I'll do my best, Walt," Fred answered very seriously, as a good skipper should. "Sure. You know that."

"You'll have to do so with this Ace Cooper fellow." Walt laughed. "I hear he's a real rip snorter, a real . . . ."

Before Walt could complete his sentence, its subject suddenly appeared by the front door coat area, smiling and carrying a large paper bag. Wanda Jeter hurried over to greet the gregarious ballplayer.

Wanda gushed. "Ace, *darling.*"

Ace planted a big kiss on Wanda's cheek, causing her to blush there in mixed company.

"Hey, baby." His voice boomed with good will and confidence. "Did you miss me? Did you miss your Ace?"

"You are so late, Ace." Wanda pretended to upbraid her young man. "Where have you been?"

"Sorry, sugar," he said slightly under his breath, just as Richard Lee Hudson came up to greet him as well, "I got, uh, delayed."

"Ace." Lee extended a big right hand, which Ace couldn't shake because of his package, "you're an absolute lifesaver."

Ace handed the other man the paper bag in lieu of the expected handshake. Despite the level of society he was entertaining this evening, Richard Lee didn't mind Ace bypassing the usual amenities. The contents of the bag meant more these days than the standard social niceties.

"How much do I owe you?"

"Twenty," Ace said.

Lee lowered his voice. "I thought it was ten."

"Risk," Ace replied.

"I only have fifteen on me."

"I'll take it," he said, "but not now. Not in front of Pete and Fred. And load your punch when no one's lookin'. I don't want to be playin' semi-pro ball next week."

Lee nodded knowingly and walked off with his sack of hooch. Ace draped a muscular arm around Wanda and gave her another big kiss.

"Why, Ace Cooper." She feigned shock in case anyone was watching. "Of all things."

"I get my money," Ace squared his shoulders as if he were about to go up to the plate and smack one out of the ballpark. "I got somethin' for you on layaway uptown."

"Oh, Ace." Wanda fluttered her eyelids sexily. "You're so silly."

"Just for you baby." He pretended—like he often and foolishly did—that he was in charge of their relationship. "Just for you."

Ace squeezed Wanda and gave her yet another kiss on the cheek. When he looked up again, Walt Harrison and Fred Casey were waving at him.

"Ace," Walt called over happily, "come on over and bring that gal of yours."

"Shit." Ace leaned over to whisper to Wanda, "Shop talk comin' up." Wanda slapped his arm as if she were offended by the language of her big strong ballplayer.

"C'mon, young feller." Fred waved to his star player. "Talk to us old timers."

"Come on, baby." Ace sighed in resignation. "It's no use. Let's go see them old buzzards."

"I want to mingle some more, honey." Wanda pouted, beautifully. "There's really important people here. You go on."

"Ah, baby...."

"Go on now." She flipped her hand off toward Fred. "Give my excuses. Tell them I have to powder my nose."

"Please, baby. Stay with me."

"Ace!" Wanda wagged a finger at the big third sacker.

"Oh, all right." Ace walked slowly over towards the baseball men, who looked dejected when they saw Wanda head off in the other direction. "Damn woman. Always on her terms. . . ."

BACK BY THE POST OFFICE

After his description of what he knew about the Richard Lee Hudson evening party and Ace Cooper's role at it, Carl continued his conversational stroll with Chief Patton.

"Well now. That's a pretty little story, but I still don't see how that gets you to this Ace boy being murdered by local shiners."

"Ace Cooper was seen leaving Ola Mae's," Carl explained patiently, "with a couple of white shiners the night he was killed."

"Oh, yeah?"

Carl eyed the policeman warily. Patton was a man of occasional surprising wit and cleverness. It was never a good idea to underestimate him nor to patronize him too obviously. He had not maintained his power over Jefferson these many years on physical threat alone. He liked to outthink his opponents, too, and adopting a country bumpkin, "shucks I don't quite get it all" attitude had worked very effectively for him in the past.

"Yes," Carl considered his answer carefully, "it looks like they were the last people to see him alive."

"You took your law course, Tatum." The chief rarely called Carl by his last name. The younger man took it as a warning. "You know that ain't no real evidence."

"They beat him and they killed him." He was becoming defensive, almost as if against his own will—and certainly against his own logic. "Then they tossed him into the alley by Ola Mae's—to make it look like a race killing."

"My God, Tatum." The chief looked at him askance. "You must hate white people with all your might. You've been treated well here in Jefferson. Why would you want to make such a claim as this?"

Carl gaped, not believing his ears. "Treated well? I'm a trained lawyer, Chief. I have a law degree from a well-known eastern school. But here in my own hometown, where I was born and raised, I have to work in a hotel doing whatever labor they let me do. I'm living day to day. I can't even get my application to take the bar examination accepted. I'm shut out of everything. You call *that* treated well?"

He knew how dangerous this was, *knew* that he was ceding the high ground, *knew* an outburst like this could cost one of his own people dearly— even if by some misdirected response by Patton. But he couldn't help himself. None of it mattered.

For his part, Patton simply leaned away from Carl and observed him like a bemused father might watch a child throwing a tantrum. "That bar thing ain't none of our doin'. That's Little Rock messin' with your lawyer test, not us. Don't I let you work for me?"

"Is that what I'm doing?" A hint of desperation crept in his voice. "Do I work for you? Am I getting paid, by the city?"

"I'll see that you get something."

"Oh, man." He shook his head.

"Now I appreciate your work, Carl. I truly do. But you've got to get better evidence 'fore I haul anybody in for that baseball player's murder."

Carl decided to play his last hole card. "Tommy Ball might see it differently."

The chief looked genuinely surprised. "Tommy Ball? Now there's no reason in the world for you to be talkin' to Tommy Ball. You're workin' for me. You keep what you know between us. Just us. Keep Ball and his do-goodin' Clean Government League out of this. They'd mess up the whole investigation. Ruin any chance of bringing the killer, or killers, to justice."

He felt the conversation righting itself. The bluff had worked. "I just want to see this through to justice same as you or anybody else."

"Sure you do." The chief smiled in agreement. "You're smart. A right thinkin' fellow. But you don't want nothin' to happen around you that would mess you up, or anybody else you know, would you?"

"Is that some kind of threat?"

The smile never wavered. "Not a bit of it. You just go about your business but keep it on the QT between me and you. No Tommy Ball. No CGL. Understand me?"

"Oh, I understand you." It would be impossible *not* to.

"Good. Now I gotta get back to the station. You take care now, Carl, and don't go jumpin' to no conclusions."

Carl stuck his hands in his pockets. "Uh-huh."

Patting the younger man on the shoulder one last time, Patton broke away and and headed off across the square. Carl shook his head and watched him go.

"Man, oh, man. This is some kind of place."

CARL TATUM

Carl Tatum was born at home, in the corrugated tin and scrap wood shed he still nominally lived in, a late arrival in the lives of Jess and Martha Tatum. Jess and Martha were nearing their fifties when the surprise of another baby caught them off guard. They themselves were both the children of slaves, people whose past had not only been torn from them and lost in the vague recollection of some now forgotten land in West Africa, but also people whose future held little, if any, hope.

Still, they had each survived impoverished growings up and had found each other when they were in their late teens. Jess was a blacksmith by trade, learned from his old daddy the slave, but mostly he survived by the sweat of his brow doing whatever labor jobs he could find in Northwest Arkansas. It was a hard enough life just to get enough money to somehow provide food and shelter for his and Martha's family, which had grown rapidly when the couple was still young.

Their first six children, though hardly provided with much more opportunity than their parents, had managed to find their own way in the world—with a couple of exceptions—and nearing mid-life, Jess and Martha were settling down to a quieter life when, as a big shock to both of them, Martha became pregnant again.

The surprise child was Carl, so called because Jess had seen that name on a grave marker at the back of the Confederate cemetery where slaves had often been interred near their owners. This unexpected boy of Jess and Martha Tatum turned out to be not only a remarkably healthy child but as time went by showed himself to be extraordinarily intelligent as well.

Jefferson's school system at the time could only be described as separate but woefully unequal and yet a small group of local youngsters managed to get at least the rudiments of an education at the all-black school there in Tin Hollow. Students went only through the eighth grade at the school, having to either move to another town with an all-black high school or, rarely, find teachers willing to tutor them in a sort of early version of home schooling.

Carl's education was of the latter variety. When his eight years at Jefferson's school for blacks ended, Mrs. Juanita Long and Brother Rodney Jackson, minister of the Black Baptist Church up on the hill by the school, combined to provide Carl with three to four hours of continued instruction right up through what would have been his high school years.

Carl worked part-time around town at whatever he could, finally getting pretty steady work at the local hotel where the owner took a liking to the bright, courteous, and respectful young man. Then, the year he turned seventeen, the most amazing thing happened to Carl Tatum.

Through the intercession of the black community in general and certain progressive elements in Jefferson, including Tommy Ball's wealthy and widowed mother, Carl was given an extraordinary opportunity. Because of the community's belief in his potential, he was able to attend Howard University, the prestigious black college located in the nation's capital. And Carl made the most of his opportunity.

He did so well, in fact, that he was given a scholarship after his freshman year and continued to receive financial aid, a portion of which he managed to save and send back home, thereby relieving some of the economic burden of his folks in Jefferson, throughout his undergraduate days and right on to the end of his law studies.

Carl worked hard all the time and was very serious. So serious that his few friends at Howard worried that he was not enjoying himself, not finding pleasure in the wonderful world that Howard and the radically buzzing east coast of the late 1920s and early 1930s had to offer.

Things were really happening for many Negroes of Carl's generation—there was the explosion of literature, art, and music of the Harlem Renaissance burning up and down the coast, there were leftist and union meetings or gatherings practically every weekend, and there were many programs and opportunities made available to blacks for the first time; opportunities that had been denied nearly the entire American black community since the painful drawing back of hope and promise after the optimistic, dreamy, and now wistful early days of the Reconstruction, which had once promised so much to America's people of color.

But while sampling all that this dynamic age had to offer, Carl had his own goals, his own concerns. Carl Tatum had a dream, an idea. He believed that if he made himself the best lawyer he could be, then he could return to his hometown and become a true champion of his people's rights, of the rights of all poor and disenfranchised people—black and white alike—he could become a force for good in the local community, he could become somebody.

The more sophisticated among his friends warned him of this dream, reminded him of his Jim Crow home, begged him to stay back east or at least in one of the bigger midwestern cities, like Chicago, where so many of their people were moving to and settling into bigger and better lives. But Carl would have none of it. He was going home and he was going to make a difference—Jim Crow be damned. Things were changing; the Roosevelts were seeing to that, and Jefferson would change, too. Everyone would see.

Only one friend stuck by Carl and his vision, a pretty, skinny girl named Dorene Masur, who was also studying to be a lawyer. Dorene and Carl often walked together on the Howard campus or on D.C.'s teeming streets, stopping at cafés to smoke cigarettes, drink coffee, and talk about their dreams. Dorene was just a year behind Carl in their studies but in her sweet, naïve disposition she seemed several years his junior. Although many on campus assumed them to be an item—they were always together and Dorene certainly wanted them to be such—Carl only considered the adoring young woman as a brilliant little sister and not as a potential partner. In the end, romance between them never budded.

When Carl returned home, they kept in touch by mail but that was all. Dorene talked of her new job as part of a legal team that occasionally provided research and briefs for Mrs. Eleanor Roosevelt herself and the dynamic young lawyer also mentioned that she was part of a southern fact-finding organization that might one day find its way to Jefferson, but so far nothing of the sort had materialized.

In the meantime, Carl found that his dream was more like a nightmare. Each year upon his return, he would apply to take the Arkansas Bar Exam, and each year his application would somehow vanish into the bowels of the apartheid bureaucracy in Little Rock. Despite his inability to get to take the Bar, Carl got noticed in Jefferson. Tommy Ball took up where his late mother had left off and became a kind of low-key champion of Carl's cause. Tommy kept trying to get Carl's application to take the Bar past the logjam in Little Rock and he occasionally found work for Carl as a sort of paralegal on minor cases.

But then in 1934, Harley Brown, a local black man, had gotten himself murdered. The local authorities, unable to penetrate the close-mouthed black community in either Ozark County or Madison County, where the suspected killers had presumably come from, had no way to solve the case. Desperate for a quick conviction to keep Tommy Ball's Clean Government League off his corruption case, Jefferson police chief Ned Patton had reluctantly taken Ball's suggestion and put Carl on the case. The logic behind Patton's move was that if the case was ever going to be solved, it would have to be done from someone inside the black community, because no one in that community trusted him, Patton, or the white power structure enough to come forward, even when threatened, cajoled, or bribed.

Using his analytical and personal skills, Carl was able to come up with the suspects in very short order—he simply followed a trail of rumor right to the scrap wood cabin where the killers had holed up in the woods not far from Huntsville, the Madison County seat. With Carl as the lead man at the trial, several witnesses corroborated the facts that Carl had gleaned, and the

Madison County killers had been tried, convicted, and sent to prison. The case made Carl a celebrity in Tin Hollow and notorious in the white community.

Despite his success and local reputation, Carl still couldn't get a job relating to the law in town and his Bar Exam application again vanished into the dark cave of Little Rock. He began to despair of ever achieving his goals; he doubted his own talent and training; he went through the drudgery of work at the hotel or wherever he could find it. He tried to keep food on his folks' table and he visited them when the spirit moved him, tending to sleep in the back of the hotel many nights as his life looked like it was stuck in a hopeless rut.

And then Robert "Ace" Cooper got himself killed and dumped at the edge of Tin Hollow near Ola Mae's. Suddenly faced with another "race" murder, Jefferson authorities needed help again. Carl was waiting and ready. This time he vowed he would do such a good job that they could no longer leave him out of their Jim Crow world. His talent and hard work would overcome all that. He would solve this case and he would get to take that damned Bar Exam. He would become a force in the community; he would become a lawyer; he would be somebody. He would. Oh, yes, he would.

DUSK IN A TIN HOLLOW DIRT ALLEY

Near sunset, Carl got off work at the hotel and headed for his folks' place. Since the Cooper killing he knew he had not been paying enough attention to his momma and daddy and so he determined to visit them this evening. He left the hotel, skirted the county courthouse, and ducked into a dirt alley at the edge of Tin Hollow. There was an old, once red brick building on his left and on the other side of the alley a rundown wooden fence that, in the places where it was still unbroken or undamaged, stood about six feet tall, just a bit above his head.

Carl was deep in thought as he walked, thinking of some way to explain his recent almost constant absence to his parents. His daddy was getting so old that the elderly man mostly just rocked in the chair Carl had bought him upon the younger man's return from the east. He hardly spoke these days and the local Baptist preacher, Brother Jackson, talked about finding the old man a place in an elderly colored folks' home down in Fort Smith. But Carl used every dime he made to help his mother buy food and necessities so that the old couple could stay in their poor little home. He couldn't imagine Jess and Martha living anywhere else.

His momma was getting up in years, too, now, and he dreaded the reality that only a few more years would bring. He pictured the little tarpaper, warped wood, and used sheet metal house empty. It wasn't an image he liked to conjure too often but he knew it would be a fact soon enough. His folks had been old when they had him and now he himself was pushing thirty.

Sighing and not paying much attention to the world around him, Carl barely noticed a sudden loud noise, like the sound of a car backfiring. He continued on down the alley for a moment, but then somewhere down deep in his consciousness the meaning of the sound registered its message and his head jerked instinctively to one side as he forced himself back into the here and now.

Slowly turning in the direction of the noise, which came from somewhere down the alley behind him, he began to react. Just as he was about to turn and fully face the alley to his rear, there was a second, louder backfire sound. Carl hunched his shoulders and swatted in the air by his own head as if a stinging insect, some species of metal bee it seemed, had flown by and almost hit him. It dawned on him then that the backfire sound wasn't coming from a car but from a gun being fired back beyond the alley. With that realization, he threw himself onto the dirt floor of the alley and up against the decaying fence.

"Son of a—"

Looking around for protection, he scrambled down the alley towards the cover of a couple of large trash cans. He rolled up behind the cans, knocking one over despite his desperate attempt to grab it before it clanged down, and sat in the dirt with his back against the brick building, waiting for the possibility of another shot. He was breathing hard but trying to keep quiet as he sat in fearful anticipation of what might come next.

For several moments he sat there, bringing his breathing under control, waiting for the expected third shot, but it did not come. Finally, he rose to one knee and took a look around the alley. There was no one to be seen. Standing slowly, he dusted himself off and then cautiously walked back up the alley to the point where he had ducked against the fence when the shooting started.

Carl carefully examined the fence and, sure enough, found where the closest of the shots had hit near the top of one of the wooden slats. There was a chipped-out place with a hole in the center, right where a small caliber round had obviously passed.

"Sweet Jesus Lord. These people."

He took a few moments to look around the vicinity for the spent shell, but because the area behind the fence was so grown up with scrub grass and weeds there was little to no chance of finding the casing or the bullet. After a brief search, he gave up.

Still a little shaken but rapidly regaining his composure, he continued on his way back down the alley towards the trash cans where he had taken momentary refuge. As he neared his temporary hiding place, something shiny and metallic in the dirt behind the overturned trash can flashed in the last light of day. Carl hustled across the alley to see what it was. As he bent down to get a better look, Dinty Blaine suddenly appeared back up at the head of the alley and called out from behind.

"Lord, young Carl." Dinty laughed nervously. "What is it now?"

Carl jumped at the sound of Dinty's voice. He had to take a moment to catch his breath before slowly turning to look back over his shoulder and speak to Dinty.

He tried to play it cool. "Hey, Dinty."

Carl used the toe of his shoe to push the shiny object behind a broken brick in the foundation of the old rundown building where the trash cans sat.

"What you doin' down there?"

"Nothin'."

"What was all that noise?"

Carl gave the old man a shrug and a smile. "It was nothing, Dinty. Just some old car backfiring, that's all."

"Lord a'mercy." He didn't sound convinced.

"I'll see you, later, Dinty," Carl said, not wanting to keep up the colloquy.

"Oh, Lord." Dinty groaned.

Without another word Carl hurried on out of the alley, making sure as he went that the shiny object he had hid could not be seen from the makeshift hiding place where he nudged it.

Back up at the top of the alley, Dinty stood for a moment watching him walk away. Then, with a shake of his head, the tired old man walked on back out of the alley and disappeared around the corner.

A VISIT WITH TOMMY BALL

The morning after Carl had been shot at back in Tin Hollow, Tommy Ball, oblivious to the previous evening's events, sat at his city hall desk poring over legal documents. He was deep into his reading, only occasionally taking a sip of coffee from a large mug beside him on the desk, when his secretary, Mary Evans, suddenly appeared in the office doorway. She had her arms spread wide in an attempt to bar someone from entering Ball's office. Ball looked up and saw Carl Tatum behind Mary's human roadblock. The boy looked very upset and was trying his best to get past her.

Mary grunted, struggling against the young man. "Mr. Ball, I tried to stop him."

Tommy Ball signaled for Mary to let Carl through. The secretary did so, reluctantly, but gave the boy a scowl of annoyance which the young man did not see as he pushed his way headlong into the room. "That's all right, Mary. It's okay. Let him pass."

She sighed. "I tried."

"You did fine." He gave her a smile, then glanced at his agitated—and slightly out of breath—visitor. "Carl Tatum, come in, come in."

"Oh, brother." With a final show of disdain, missed by both men, the secretary turned and stomped back out to her desk in the outer office.

"What can I do for you?"

The boy looked like he hadn't slept. His eyes were bloodshot and his clothes rumpled. "I was walking in the hollow last night, minding my own business, and somebody took a shot at me."

Tommy held up a hand to signal for silence, then got up and walked past him to close the office door.

"Shot at you?" Tommy settled back into his big, comfortable leather-backed chair. "You say somebody took a shot at you? With a gun?"

"With a gun they did, yes, sir." Carl nodded excitedly. "Yes, they sure as hell did. Over in that dirt alley by the old cleaning supply building. The bullet knocked a hole in the wood fence across from there."

"Well, I—" Tommy rubbed his chin. "Whoever would have . . . ."

"You have to do something right now, Mr. Ball." Carl still hadn't sat down. "I ain't going to get myself killed over this white boy's murder. I don't even know what's going on here. I'm getting caught between the no-good moonshiners and the no-good law, if there's a difference. Damn, I ain't so sure the chief didn't do this shooting at me himself or at least have somebody do it for him. I know he's playing me some way or the other."

The councilman smiled wryly. "Well, now, you know that's for sure. You bet he is. He's a sly one, old Patton. The corrupt bastard. We been trying to get him out of office for over two years."

"I wish you'd get him out right now."

"But, can't you see? You're obviously on the right track. If people are taking potshots at you, I mean."

"Maybe I need to get off that track." He blew out a breath. "Right now. I don't know why I help these people anyway. It never gets me anywhere."

Visions of a Patton-less Jefferson danced through Ball's head for a moment, and he had to take a deep breath to keep his enthusiasm in check. "You help because that's the kind of man you are. A good citizen. Not like the Pattons and their ilk—trying to ruin Jefferson with their thievin' and corruption. They're exactly the kind of people President and Mrs. Roosevelt, Lord bless 'em, want us to root out, to clear out, so that the country can get back on its feet again. To be strong and clean and proud. That's the kind of America we want, the kind of Jefferson we want, and need, and deserve."

Carl grunted. He'd heard this song and dance a million times before from white folks. Everything was New Deal this and New Deal that. He wondered when his people would ever get their New Deal.

"We may just have a chance here." Tommy thumped the top of the desk with his fist. "A chance to knock these people down. Help me get Patton, Carl. Help me bring that bastard down."

"I don't know." He was pretty uncomfortable listening to Ball's quasi-religious fervor. In the short term, he just wanted some protection.

"It could mean a lot to you."

"How so?"

"You're an ambitious man, Carl," Tommy said, sure of his ground. "One who wants to get ahead in life. Better his station. Be a credit to his community and race."

Carl held his chin with his thumb and first finger. "Uh-huh."

"We all know you're a smart n—uh, fellow. We all know you want to be a lawyer."

"Uh-huh."

Tommy stated the obvious fact. "But your application to take the bar exam never seems to get far in Little Rock?"

He shook his head. "Huh-uh."

Tommy gestured expansively. "So that's what I can do for you. I can get you off high center. Get you a chance to take the bar exam. And if you're as sharp as we all think you are, that's your shot at the big target. Your chance to serve your community, to support the law, to be the kind of American the Roosevelts say all of us can be—regardless of race, color, or creed."

"You can do that for me?" Carl's mind whirled. Could Ball really deliver on such a promise? "You said you could before but—"

"I *will* do that for you. This time it's a done deal. And don't forget, I've got friends in the federal government. Good friends. And when this town is ours, there will be jobs for those who helped us. Good jobs."

"You promise?" Carl's hopes soared, his long-awaited dream swimming in the forefront of his consciousness. All he wanted was a chance in life. A chance to make a good living, a chance to be part of the community, a chance to help other people.

"I promise," Tommy said, raising his right hand to God.

"Swear on a bible?"

"Whatever."

"All right, then." He moved up closer to the councilman, who sat back in his chair. "I'm your man. I'll tell you what I've learned so far."

CARL AND DINTY AT OLA MAE'S

On the previous Saturday night at Ola Mae's juke joint, after the near run-in with the tough bloods over the attentions of Vera Cottey, Carl had taken Dinty Blaine into the backroom office to grill the older man about what he knew concerning the events of the night Ace Cooper was killed. As usual, Dinty was reluctant to tell what he knew, but Carl's knack for getting people to open up had had its impact and the old man began to talk.

"Now, young Carl," Dinty said after reassurance that no one was going to "get" him for just talking about Ace Cooper's death. "You know I avoids white people trouble like the plague. I don't want to see or hear nothin'. Each to his own—that's what my old daddy used to say. He was a good man."

"I know he was, Dinty. I remember him from when I was a little boy."

"He was real old then."

He nodded, anxious to keep the cook talking. "Yes, he was."

"And I told that police chief that, too," Dinty said, a little defensively. "I don't see or know nothin'. I listen to my daddy."

"That's smart. But how can a man avoid white people trouble when it's all around him?" Carl shook his head. "You work for those people. And the baseball boys come around here at Ola Mae's. You've seen what they do."

"I seen more'n I want," Dinty allowed.

"I bet you have. And you not wanting to get mixed up in it and all."

"That's right."

He kept Dinty moving forward, following the bread crumbs. "But a man like you, one everybody knows works real hard and does a good job. A man they all trust. You get in places you can't miss what's going on."

"Lord, ain't that the truth," Dinty shook his head again.

"Like this Cooper fellow. You found his body. Poor man."

"Yes I did. I should never have gone out into that alley again."

"But you have to. It's your job. Ola Mae's trash has got to be dumped."

Dinty frowned. "Got to be."

"Gotta go in that alley." He nodded again, like a church acolyte during a Sunday sermon. Sing it, brother. "Every night. Couple of times a night."

"More 'n once."

"Can't help but see stuff that way."

"I didn't want to see nothin'."

"Naw."

"Naw. But it was all night long."

"All night long?" Carl gave the old man a doubting look.

Dinty saw it and raised a hand, palm out. "Straight gospel. First they was them white boys. Them mean-ass shiners. You know the ones."

"Uh-huh." Carl motioned for him to continue.

"I just poked my head around the corner."

"You couldn't help but hear." He paused for a beat. "And see?"

"A little."

DINTY SEES MORE THAN HE SHOULD

Working from memory of the events he observed concerning the fate of Ace Cooper, Dinty described for Carl what he saw as he peered around a corner in the alley by Ola Mae's on that now memorable night. It was dark outdoors but there was enough light for the old man to have recognized Wade Smith and his enforcer, Mack, standing there in the alley.

"I'm good for it, fellows," Dinty recalled hearing Ace say to the moonshiners. "You know I am."

"Forty bucks," Wade Smith had countered. "We want it now, baseball boy."

"I need a couple of days. C'mon."

"Now," Smith said.

Ace held up his hands. "I ain't got it now. I only got five."

Without another word, Smith and Mack jumped on him and began pummeling him. At first they were only slapping him around, but as Ace tried to resist, the two toughs started giving him a real beating. Mack held the ballplayer up while Smith unloaded hard, unblocked punches at his upper body and face.

"You'll never cheat us again, you pissant," Smith growled.

Ace grunted and moaned under the assault. "Stop."

"Get his money," Smith told Mack. The big hooligan dug through Ace's clothes and came up with the five.

He held it up. "Five lousy bucks. Just like he said."

Smith snorted and spat on Ace's shirt. "You better get the rest by tomorrow, asshole. Or we'll come lookin' for you again."

To punctuate the threat, the pair hammered Ace several times more. Ace's face was a swollen, bloody pulp. Mack grabbed the ballplayer and stood him up one more time so that Smith could cold-cock him with a powerful right cross. Ace fell face first in the alley like a dead, bloody tree.

"That ought to get the message home." Smith chuckled. "Let's get out of here."

Just as the two hoodlums began to move off, they heard a door close nearby. With a start they looked around for the source of the sound.

"Somebody seen us," Mack said.

"Who gives a damn?"

"It was probably that goddamned Dinty Blaine over at Ola Mae's. That old son of a bitch is always stickin' his nose in everywhere."

"Don't matter." Smith raised his voice, loud enough so Dinty could hear. "Dinty Blaine knows better than to say anything. He knows we'll shut him up for good if he does."

"Here's the fiver." Mack handed over the bill he'd taken from Ace Cooper.

Smith grabbed the five-spot. "Let's go."

CARL AND DINTY BACK AT OLA MAE'S

Carl listened patiently to Dinty's story, but when it was over he had more questions for the old man.

"Did you go out to see what happened, Dinty?"

"No, sir, young Mr. Carl. I run back into work."

"You didn't know if this fellow was dead or alive?"

Dinty shook his head. "No, sir."

"You didn't come out again until you found the body next morning?"

"I, uh...."

Carl's eyebrows went up. "Dinty, did something else happen that night? You saw something else?"

The old cook avoided his gaze. "I don't want to say, Mr. Carl."

He sighed. "Dinty, this is important. Please, help me here. This man was murdered. What else did you see?"

"Well. . . ."

DINTY GETS MORE THAN HE BARGAINED FOR

Dinty had waited twenty minutes or more after the white toughs knocked Ace Cooper senseless before he got up the gumption to try and take out the garbage again. He very carefully and slowly opened Ola Mae's back door, pausing to look around and to listen. There was no sound.

Slowly, he stepped out into the alley and peeked around the corner.

There was a heavy groan from the prostrate figure there in the alley. Dinty instinctively recoiled, but then started to go on, feeling he had to at least check on the body there; but just as he was about to move forward, he heard someone else coming into the alley. The old man froze in his tracks.

A dark figure appeared and walked up to where Cooper lay in pain. He—Dinty was at least certain about that part—reached down grabbed a handful of the injured ballplayer's hair.

"You rotten white son of a bitch." It was a deep voice, familiar to the old cook. "I teach you mess around with what's mine."

Dinty watched and listened in terror as the figure spat in Ace's face and then began digging through the battered man's clothes. Finding nothing, he then reached down and pulled Ace's shoes off. Dinty could barely make out something that the man had extracted from one of the shoes and now held in his hands.

"Cheatin', lyin' bastard. I knowed you would have money on you somewhere. A tenner."

Ace struggled against the man then, tried to get up and fight, but the assailant punched him hard to the body. Cooper dropped to his knees. The dark figure produced a knife and without pause stabbed him several times. The ballplayer fell forward, dead in the alley.

The killer looked up at the sound of a door quickly closing. "Who's there? Ola Mae? Dinty? Dinty Blaine? Is that you, Dinty Blaine? I'll get you, you old son of a bitch."

LAST CALL AT OLA MAE'S

The old man seemed to have finally finished his story.

"That's all? There isn't anything else?"

"That's all they is."

"Oh, my God, Dinty." Carl whistled, eyes wide in disbelief. "Why didn't you tell me this before?"

"I don't want no trouble. I just don't want none."

Carl sighed and rubbed his chin. Dinty's information had hit him like a small bombshell. He was having trouble putting it in its proper place. It turned his current thinking on its head. "Oh, man."

"What you gonna do, Carl?"

He thought about it for a minute. "I don't have much choice."

"You have to leave white folks stuff alone, boy." Dinty shook his head. "Just leave it be."

"It's all right, Dinty. You won't have any trouble."

"You be careful now, son. You walk easy."

"I will, Dinty. I will. Don't you worry."

Without another word, Carl got up and walked out of Ola Mae's. Dinty stayed seated where he was.

ROBERT "ACE" COOPER

Robert Cooper was born in the midst of his family's six siblings. He was the fourth child, including two lost to miscarriage, and the second son. Like most mid-family children, especially boys, Robert was basically ignored. His older brother John, the first born, was the family's shining light and his two older sisters, pretty and smart, were doted on by their father, a seldom-home drummer who sold anything he could for anyone he could throughout mid-western Illinois and mid-eastern Missouri. Billy, Robert's little brother by two years, and Mary, the baby in the family and nearly four years younger than Robert, were both spoiled rotten by both their parents and the older brothers and sisters.

To get attention, Robert compensated by becoming a very rowdy, troublesome boy. At school he was always being sent to stand in the corner of the room for talking out loud during class or punching a fellow student or pulling a girl's braids. At home it was lots of extra chores to punish him for his steady stream of practical jokes, rude comments, and "bad doings" as his weary mother usually referred to them. He looked for all the world like the kind of boy who was heading straight to reform school until about age twelve. That was when Robert Cooper made the most important discovery of his life: he was a natural athlete.

Suddenly he was transformed, not into an upright citizen, dedicated student, or prize child, but into an athlete, a really, *really*, good one. Robert could play anything and play it well. He became quarterback on the school football team, the center in basketball, and a pitcher and centerfielder on the baseball team. He would have done more but the big three sports were basically all that were offered at little Carlton, Illinois high school.

With his prowess in sports Robert and his world changed. He became confident, even cocky. His teammates took to calling him "Ace" because of his extraordinary skill, and people he didn't even know complimented him and respected him. It was his immediate salvation from the unfruitful path he had been following for most of his life. And there was one other big change in Robert's life: the girls in Carlton liked him.

And Ace found that he liked the girls, too. In fact, he liked them a lot. He liked to buy them things. Especially pretty things to wear. He liked them to look really good and he liked for people to know that they were his girls. The more he dealt with girls and women, the more Ace realized that he liked the challenge of going after and then keeping the one considered the best of the best, the pick of the litter, the queen of the hop.

Because he had never thought he could accomplish anything before in his ignored life, Ace found that he was now stimulated and excited by this process of going after the unattainable—going after it and then holding on to it at whatever cost. It became a part of who the young man was.

There was the high school cheerleader, and the smartest girl in school, then—as he got older—the prettiest divorcee in town, and then the wife of the richest man, and on and on. It was a pattern Ace would repeat in several locations as the budding young athlete finished school, tried out with the St. Louis Cardinals baseball team, and finally got assigned to their farm system as a prospect.

Jefferson, Arkansas, in the tiny Class D Ozark Mountain League, was Ace's second stop in the Cardinals' organization. He had done very well playing for the Beatrice Blues in the Nebraska State League, a Class D league like the Ozark. Ace had torn up the pitching in Nebraska and had been among the league's leading hitters. He had also blossomed into a fine fielder, becoming a strong-armed, sometimes exceptional third baseman.

Ace hoped to move up fast in the Cardinals chain and at Jefferson once more he was at the very top of the league in hitting, homeruns, RBIs, and fielding. At mid-season, he had been assured by none other than Branch Rickey himself—who very, *very* occasionally made the trip down to watch the little Ozark Mountain League and its budding Cardinals players—that he, Ace, would be promoted to Class C Springfield, Missouri by the end of the year and with a shot at even higher leagues the following season. With that bit of news in his pocket, a confident Ace went about the business of pursuing a more specific goal.

Early in the current season, he had met and at least temporarily won the attentions of his latest erstwhile unattainable object, the pretty and rather materially-oriented Miss Wanda Jeter. Even though Jefferson was to Ace a podunk town, Wanda herself was the most difficult woman he had yet encountered. For she was a big city girl living in a small town world. Wanda was prone to give her attentions in a most erratic, mercurial way and this often threw Ace off his game.

Wanda was also very keen on the finer things in life and expected any beau of hers to provide them, with very little complaint. It was unsightly to worry about such things as prices and bills. In addition, Wanda made it clear to any man who might court her that she was a thing of rare value, well worth holding on to, and not something to be trifled with. Ace Cooper agreed with her lavish assessment of herself and her personal worth.

To keep Wanda as his own, in a town filled with rakes ready to step into his shoes should he stumble for even a moment, Ace began to spend well beyond the salary he made monthly from the Jefferson Redbirds. Wanda required constant material reinforcement of both her personal value to Ace and of his devotion to her. Ace was bound and determined not to let her down. But keeping up with Miss Wanda Jeter and holding on to her soon taxed Ace to the limit and that was when he made his biggest mistake: he began to sell moonshine on the side for extra money.

As a popular player on the only local professional baseball team, Ace had quickly made lots of new acquaintances in Jefferson, and as a handsome, personable young man he was soon able to move into some of the better circles in town as well. There he found willing customers for his new sidelight as moonshine middleman, people who had a few bucks to spend and a thirst for home brew.

The fly in Ace's ointment, however, turned out to be Wanda. She kept spending every dime Ace could scrounge together and more, and soon the zealous to please ballplayer found himself seriously overextended financially—actually owing money to his moonshine suppliers, both black and white—and that got him into trouble. That and a new taste Ace acquired in the back streets of Jefferson.

Wanda Jeter was a beautiful woman and she liked to be decked out to the nines, but she didn't have the same extravagance when it came to offering her physical wares or to satisfying Ace's more basic needs. In fact, she wouldn't put out at all for Ace and the fine young third sacker was driven nearly to distraction by it.

The solution Ace found was in some local black establishments where white boys with money were usually welcomed by the cash-strapped owners and by some of the feminine customers, most notably the earthy and sensuous Vera Cottey, who seemed to take a special liking to Ace Cooper and who was not adverse to satisfying some of the ballplayer's more natural impulses.

So Ace found his solace with willing local black girls, mostly Vera, and ran up a huge debt keeping his virginal white girlfriend in all the fine clothes she could purchase at the stores up on Jefferson's quaint square; and he got himself deeper and deeper in the red with his moonshine sources.

Finally, in the heat of a Northwest Arkansas August, all of those elements had come into play and the result was Robert "Ace" Cooper's inert body lying face down in a pool of blood in a dirty little alley in an impoverished little town in the middle of nowhere. Another potentially fine athletic career and life wasted on the way. Robert "Ace" Cooper, third sacker for the local nine, was dead, murdered in the back streets of a backwater town in a backwater region of the country. A forgotten man in a forgotten time and place.

AT WADE SMITH'S GARAGE

One hot afternoon, Wade Smith and his main mechanic, Mack, were hard at work inside Smith's garage while outside, R. J. Jones, the other mechanic—a skinny counterpoint to Mack's beefiness—was breaking down a tire to repair it. R. J. tried his best to find shade while he worked but it was deep enough into the day to make that a mostly a futile attempt. Inside was hardly better as the still air and confined quarters, while better than being in the direct sun, combined to make work in the garage bays a sweaty, sticky, and pretty miserable proposition.

Stepping away for a moment from the engine he and Smith were working on, big Mack wiped the perspiration from his forehead with a dirty shop rag just as the Jefferson Police patrol car pulled up in front of the garage. The mechanic could see Chief Ned Patton behind the wheel of the vehicle, accompanied by Patrolman Roy Holmes. Mack tapped Smith on the shoulder and nodded his head at the arriving car.

"There's the law." Smith looked up and outside at the police car. Holmes already had his door part way open before the chief shut the vehicle off.

"So to speak," Smith grumbled to Mack's snickering laugh.

Smith slowly stepped away from the car they were working on and, taking the dirty shop rag from Mack to make a pretense at cleaning his hands, sauntered out to meet the police.

As he passed R.J. outside, Smith signaled to the heavily sweating boy. "Go get the chief a cold co-cola out of the ice box, boy, and bring it to him."

"You want one, too?"

"Naw."

When Smith was within a few feet of the patrol car, Chief Patton slowly piled out of the car to join Patrolman Holmes by the curb. The two lawmen casually walked up to Smith.

The chief dabbed his forehead with a handkerchief. "What ya say, Smith?"

"'Fraid to say it, Chief." Smith smiled crookedly.

"Looks like you're keepin' busy." Chief Patton swept his arm around, taking in the garage environs where several other cars waited for the mechanics' attention.

"Got no complaints."

R.J. arrived with the chief's soft drink. The chief took the cola and downed a big slug without any pretense of paying for it. "Mighty refreshin'. It's powerful hot out today."

Smith jerked a thumb up and R.J. hustled back inside the shop to help Mack. Patrolman Holmes looked like he was about to say something, but held back.

The chief smirked. "Got another one of these cold pops for old Roy here?"

Without looking at Holmes, Smith silently pointed back at the garage.

"You don't mind gettin' your own, Roy?" Chief Patton asked his underling with no hint of irony.

Holmes grunted. Despite his obvious minding, the patrolman headed on into the garage for his own pop.

"Let's talk under this shade tree," Smith suggested to the chief when Holmes was gone. Together, they walked over into the shade of a huge old oak.

"With a little wind," the chief said between pulls on his soda bottle, "this'd be downright tolerable."

Smith decided to get down to the business he knew had to be behind the chief's rare visit to the garage. "Social visit, chief? Or business?"

"Well, Wade," Patton smiled in a relaxed, friendly way, and tipped his hat back on his head, "I was actually just wonderin' if you been troublin' that black boy I got workin' for me?"

"Black boy?" Smith asked, playing it a little cagey with the chief, as befit their extra-legal relationship.

"You know." Patton looked away. "That Tatum boy. Carl."

"What about him?" Smith's yardbird hackles began to rise.

"I was concerned that he might have, uh, stepped over his bounds a bit and that you might have tried to, maybe, redirect his efforts of late."

"What in the hell are you talkin' about, Patton?" Smith's no nonsense approach to life came to the fore despite the chief's power and authority. "Speak straight."

The chief's voice stayed icy-cool and calm. "You try to shoot that boy the other evenin'?"

"What?" Smith laughed. "If I'd tried to shoot his black ass, he'd be dead."

"You never . . . ?"

"Hell, no." Smith blew air out the side of his mouth. "You ought to be gettin' him off this here thing anyways, if you get my meanin'. The boy might could find stuff out he don't need to know."

"Uh-huh. You sure you never done nothin'?"

"You'd know if I'd done somethin'." Smith shook his head. "He'd know."

"Then who?"

As the chief pondered his own question, Patrolman Holmes began walking back out from the garage, sipping on his own soft drink, heading for the shade tree. The chief looked at Smith.

"Who do you—" Smith began.

"Never mind."

Smith turned then and looked at Holmes just as the patrolman rejoined them. Smith and Patton exchanged a quick glance.

"What?" Holmes saw the look that passed between the two men. "What?"

"Nothin'." Chief Patton adjusted his hat again. "We was just jawin'."

Smith laughed.

Holmes looked confused. Chief Patton took another slug from his soda. Smith suddenly reached over and tapped the chief on the shoulder.

"Yeah?"

Smith nodded towards the street. Patton turned to see Wanda Jeter swishing her way up the narrow sidewalk that ran in front of Smith's garage.

"Lookie there." Smith leered at the pretty woman.

Holmes groaned. "Oh, man."

The chief handed Holmes what was left of his soda, leaving the patrolman holding a bottle of pop in each hand. "Steady, hoss. You just cool off."

"A woman like that ought'n to have to be walkin' on a hot day like today," the chief declared, then raised his voice to address Wanda. "Excuse me, Miss Jeter?"

Holmes looked confused. "But, Chief, how'll I get back to the station?"

"For cryin' out loud, Holmes," Patton said over his shoulder, "get a ride with one of Smith's boys."

Holmes looked lost and hurt. Smith shook his head in disgust. To the hardcore ex-con, Patrolman Roy Holmes was the worst kind of sissy pissant in the world.

Holmes put on his best authoritarian front. "I want to go right now, Smith."

Smith laughed. "You'll go when one of my boys has time to take you, Holmes. Simple as that."

Holmes sighed in resignation. Out at the curb, the patrolman could see that Chief Patton had stopped Wanda Jeter. Holmes turned away and went inside the garage, sipping from both bottles of pop.

On the street, the chief continued glad-handing Wanda. "May I give you a lift uptown, Miss Jeter?"

Wanda smiled at him demurely. "Why, Chief, that would be marvelous. It's a terrible hot day."

"Yes, ma'am, it is. Please allow me."

The chief gallantly opened the rider's side door to let Wanda into the patrol car. He ogled a trim, shapely leg as Wanda sat down in the car. The chief closed the door after Wanda and, with a little smile back at the garage, hustled around to the driver's side of the vehicle. Both Smith and Holmes were watching as the chief started the patrol car and drove away towards uptown.

Smith smiled coarsely. "Old Chiefie, always schemin'."

Mack and R.J. snickered.

"Disgusting," Holmes sniffed.

Smith looked over at him and laughed. "Only 'cause you ain't gettin' any."

Holmes turned and silently walked away.

Smith spat into the dirt in the spot vacated by the patrolman.

CHIEF NED PATTON

Ned Patton was the son of a Jefferson police officer. His father, Arlen, had served on the force during the early part of the century and had acquired a reputation for being a tough but fair man. Arlen Patton had worked hard for the citizens of Jefferson. He had to, with a family of seven—five girls and two boys—to feed, clothe, and house. To augment his income, Arlen did occasionally dip his hand into the police till—an unreported fine here, a spare, free meal there, but all in all he was a decent man and a good officer of the law.

Arlen's oldest son, Ned, a big, strapping bully of a boy, at first showed no interest in his father's profession, or in pursuing it himself. Ned was content to push smaller boys around, torment girls, and take things that he or the family couldn't afford. Late in his teens, as he was about to finish up a less than illustrious high school career, Ned finally pushed his luck just a bit too far.

Late one Saturday evening, he and a couple of his chums decided it would be a good idea to take the day's receipts from the little old man who ran the Bijou Theatre, Jefferson's oldest and poorest movie house. When the boys were caught less than a half hour after the heist, they were brought into the Jefferson police station and booked on theft charges. Due to the influence of Ned's father, the charges were dropped for all the boys, but the old man decided that as far as his son went it was time for a change.

Using reverse psychology, Arlen Patton talked his chief into hiring Ned Patton on the police force. The idea, not so uncommon in those days, was that it was better to have the boy working for the law where he could be watched and perhaps controlled rather than to leave him unattended and to his own devices.

At first the plan worked fine. Young Ned took to police work like a duck to water. As a junior patrolman, he could now legally and officially bully people around, fine them—often for no reason whatsoever—and in no time he learned to use his position to help and protect his group of pals, one of whom, a very rough character named Wade Smith, had returned to Jefferson about that time after spending a couple of years in the Arkansas State penitentiary.

Ned Patton also found that his position of authority allowed him to coerce women into "compromising" situations and he used this power as often as he was able. Even better for the budding young lawman was the advent of Prohibition. With the outlawing of alcohol, moonshine liquor— made and distributed illegally—became one of the major sources of revenue in the area, especially after the crash of the stock market and the burden of the depression that followed.

Arlen Patton retired in 1930 and his boy Ned was ready not only to replace his father on the force but to make his move to take over the entire police department as well. Ned ran a very rough campaign for the position of police chief, using threats and photographic blackmail to discredit and defeat his rival for the job. His brother Martin rode the older sibling's coat tails into the County Assessor's office and the real Patton era in Jefferson began.

Within a year of his election, Ned Patton had consolidated his power over the town through a program of harassment, physical intimidation, and open corruption. He was up to his ears in moonshining, women, extortion, and stolen automobiles. By 1932 he was the most powerful individual in Ozark County. Ned Patton ruled Jefferson and its immediate area with a strong, sometimes punishing, arm. He made a lot of money and he began to conversely make a lot of enemies.

Although he had terrorized almost all of genteel Jefferson, Patton did have some people who actively fought back against his domineering ways and autocratic rule. A group calling itself the Clean Government League, headed up by energetic local lawyer and city councilman Tommy Ball, began to try to unseat Patton legally. The CGL filed lawsuits on behalf of Jefferson's citizenry attempting to prove that Patton was corrupt and involved in illegal activities up to his ears—which he was.

In the early thirties, as the depression deepened and spread around the country, the era of the midwestern outlaw began. Around the Ozarks this new type of criminal was represented by such characters as Charles "Pretty Boy" Floyd and the infamous Barrow Gang. Wade Smith, Patton's "silent" partner in local "business" dealings, knew both Floyd and W.D. Jones of the Barrow outfit and often provided them with one of his "appropriated" vehicles.

The CGL, getting wind of such activities, went after Ned Patton through his connection to Smith and they tried their best to unseat the powerful chief of police. But Patton still had a solid base of coerced support among the many citizens and entrepreneurs that he pushed around on a daily basis and despite several injunctions and two trials aimed at deposing the chief, Patton managed to maintain his control over the local community. But as the 30s moved along, his position became more and more precarious.

By 1935, Ned Patton was still very powerful in Jefferson but the efforts of the CGL, declining public support for the chief, and a more critical legal system had eroded his power to the point that he, his brother Martin, and their cronies were only one or two more mistakes from being unseated. With the CGL and its supporters steadily coming after him, Patton began to feel picked upon, under pressure, a little desperate. He fought hard to control his town but he sometimes had a sinking feeling that it was getting away from him. All that was needed, he feared, was one more big event, or error, and he would be out.

Then, in the summer of 1935, Robert "Ace" Cooper, local pro baseball player and bon vivant, turned up dead in the colored section of town. It was just what Patton didn't need and it was just what his opponents had been waiting for. How

Ned Patton handled the investigation, how it was resolved, would go a long way in determining if his era of one man authority was at an end.

Patton knew he had to find a way to sweep the Cooper murder under a metaphorical rug. With the continuation of his power in mind, Patton enlisted the aid of people no one else would touch and he hit on a final scheme to control the situation should it not turn out the way he had planned. With the summer of 1935 moving towards its end, Ned Patton was ready to make a last stand to maintain his hold on tiny Jefferson, Arkansas.

How that stand would turn out remained to be seen. It was up in the air. But one thing was for certain, Ned Patton would not go down without a major fight. He might fall, but many others would go with him—including both friends and enemies. The end of the Ned Patton era in Jefferson promised to be a messy one, if not downright bloody and vicious.

CARL FINDS TREASURE

Early on a clear, as yet cool morning, Carl Tatum walked briskly towards the Ozark Hotel where he was scheduled to work the early morning shift. As he neared the edge of Tin Hollow, he abruptly turned to his right and detoured from his normal route. Looking around to see if anyone was watching, he slipped into the dirt alley where he had hidden the shiny object just after whoever had taken the shots at him a couple of days before.

Cautiously making his way down the alley, he easily found the broken brick where he had pushed the object into hiding with his shoe. Bending down, he dug around the brick and then loosened it. Reaching in back of the brick, he found the object and held it up to better see what it was.

It was a knife, a Barlow knife, in fact—extremely common for the time, lots of boys and men had them—but this one seemed to have some kind of engraving on it that had been scratched on rather than professionally done. Closely examining the knife, Carl recoiled when he saw what appeared to be dried blood along the edge of the blade.

"Uh-oh."

Carefully dusting off the knife, Carl took care not to knock off any of the dried blood. He took a handkerchief from his shirt pocket, wrapped the knife in it, and was just about to delicately stash the package in his trousers when he became aware that he was no longer alone in the alley. Looking up, he saw, not twenty feet away and coming down the alley towards him, Wade Smith's mechanics, R.J. and Mack.

"Oh, shit." He quickly finished dropping the handkerchief-wrapped knife into his pants pocket. The toughs came right up to him, and Carl assumed a ready-to-fight-but-not-belligerent stance towards them.

"What you doin', Tatum?" big Mack wanted to know.

Carl jerked his head up the hill. "Headin' to work."

R.J. rubbed his nose and snickered. "Oh, yeah?"

Carl ignored him.

Mack cocked his head to one side. "Where you work, boy?"

"You know very well I work at the hotel."

"Oh, yeah?"

Carl glanced at R.J. and shook his head in disdain. The redneck made as if to hit him, but Mack held him back with a thick arm.

"Easy, R.J. This boy just needs a talkin' to, not an ass whuppin'.""

His ears perked up. "What's that supposed to mean? Who sent you?"

"You never mind about that," Mack said.

"Then get out of my way and let me go on to work." He moved to brush past them, but Mack blocked his path. Carl took a step back and raised his fists. "Step back. I won't say it again."

The big man ignored the defensive posture. "Listen, Tatum. We just got one message for you."

"And what would that be?"

R.J. pushed forward again, and again Mack held him back. Carl looked straight into R.J.'s face, as if inviting the tough to take a swing at him.

Mack held up his arms between them, keeping the two men at arm's length. "You'd be smart to take it easy on what you diggin' around about."

Carl shook his head. This wasn't the first run-in he'd had with these two crackers, and they should know by now he wasn't one to be trifled with. They'd both taken their share of licks from him in their tussles. "I'm working for the city authorities, not whoever sent you two. And if you people have something to hide, don't think threatening me will make me stop trying to find out who killed that baseball man. I know he was mixed up in dirty white people's business."

With Carl's declaration, R.J. lunged towards him again. Carl drew back his right arm, ready to strike.

"Who you callin' dirty, nigger?" R. J. snarled.

"Easy, R.J." Mack gave a little laugh. He moved the lighter mechanic away from Carl with one of his massive arms. "Easy. Ain't no reason to get all riled up."

"Shit." R. J. spat down onto the dirt of the alley. The hatred in his eyes burned deep, hot, and red.

"You need to keep your dog on a leash."

Mack remained implacable. "Never mind about that, Tatum. This is the last thing I have to say to you. Walk careful, boy, very careful. And as far as that dead man goes, you'd be smarter to maybe look closer to home 'fore you go blamin' everthing on white people."

"You—" Carl stopped, brought up short by the big man's suggestion as to just exactly who killed Ace Cooper. "I—I'll find out my own facts."

It was weak, and he knew it. But it was all he could come up with on the fly.

Mack smirked. "Just don't let all the white skin you're seein' blind you to them facts you so proud of findin'."

Without another word, the big mechanic turned and, dragging the frothing R.J. with him, walked away. All the way out of the alley, R.J. kept turning back and giving him the evil eye, but Carl ignored him. He was pondering things of far greater import than the open racism and threatening hostility of two dirty rednecks.

CALLING AT THE COTTEY RESIDENCE

Carl Tatum stood staring at Henry Cottey's front door as if trying to make up his mind whether to knock on it or not. Finally he did knock. Softly at first, then harder and louder.

After a few moments, Vera Cottey appeared at the door. She wore a cotton dress that left little of her body's form to the imagination. Carl had to make an effort not to be distracted by this most pleasurable sight.

"Good day to you, Miss Vera." He kept his voice cool and proper.

"Why, Carl Tatum." A natural sexuality coated her each and every word. "How you doin', sugar?"

"I'm doin' just fine. May I ask if your father is home?"

"May you ask?" Vera laughed, her voice ringing clean and happy in the air. "My father? You are such a formal boy, Carl. You come here to see him and not me?"

"Yes, miss."

"And callin' me 'miss.'" Vera shook her head. "My, my."

"Who that knockin'?" a heavy, masculine voice called out from inside the house.

"Now look what you done." Vera smiled seductively. "You done got my daddy all jumped up in there."

"Vera!" Henry Cottey's voice boomed from inside again, "who at the door?"

"It's Carl Tatum, daddy," Vera called back over her shoulder. "You know, that good lookin' lawyer boy."

Vera reached out and ran a finger suggestively down Carl's chest. He looked at her finger and his shirt. From within the house, there was a lot of banging around and then Henry Cottey's fearsome visage appeared behind Vera in the doorway.

"What you want here, boy?"

Carl steeled himself against the older man's aggressive hostility.

"I have some questions I want to ask you, Mr. Cottey."

"Questions? What questions?"

"We should talk alone," Carl suggested, looking at Vera. She winked and smiled sweetly at him.

"Go ahead and talk, that girl don't pay no never mind."

He took a breath. "You may not like it."

"I don't like it already. Say what you got to say and get on with it."

"All right. What do you know about that white baseball man got killed up by Ola Mae's?"

"White baseball man?" Cottey looked away. "Who you mean? I don't know nothin'."

Carl clenched and unclenched his jaw, working to keep his temper. "Robert Cooper was his name. They called him Ace. The one they found his body by Ola Mae's. He used to hang out there sometimes. Maybe sold some 'shine around town."

Vera nodded. "I remember him. He was a sweet boy. Nice to me."

"He was nothin' but trouble." Cottey frowned. "Come messin' 'round black folks."

"You did know him then. And what trouble was that he was into?"

"Everbody know him." The old man gave out a harsh laugh, almost like a bark. "Sumbitch white boy owed everbody in town money. White shiners, me— probably the law. He stealin' off the top o' all us."

Carl jumped on that. "Is that why he got killed?"

Cottey cast a wary eye his way. "I didn't say nothin' 'bout that."

"Lot of people might want to hurt him?"

"Might." Cottey looked down at his worn, dirty boots.

"Not me," Vera said brightly. "He was cute. And nice."

"Shut up," the old man told his daughter. "Or I take a strap to you."

Carl blew out a breath in frustration. "This Ace stole from you then, is that what you're telling me?

"I done said that."

"Make you mad enough to hurt this boy?"

Cottey's hackles were well up by this time. He pushed past Vera to stand squarely in the center of the doorway. "Why you askin'? You ain't no police."

Carl stood his ground. "No, I'm not. But somebody hurt him bad and then somebody—maybe somebody else—killed him. With a knife."

Vera shook her pretty head. "Oh, how terrible."

Her father said nothing.

"You own a knife, Mr. Cottey?" Carl asked, as offhanded as he could.

Cottey cocked his head. "Everbody do."

"But you like special ones. Barlow's. Right?"

"Um...." It could have been interpreted as a yes or a no.

"You have your knife with you now?"

"I don't know."

Carl sensed a chink in the moonshiner's fearsome defenses. The harsh old man seemed a little confused. "You always scratch your initials on your knives?"

"You gettin' at somethin'?"

"I found a Barlow knife near where that white man was killed." He crossed his arms across his chest, as though deep in thought. "It had blood on it. Dried blood. And some letters were scratched on the blade."

Suddenly Henry Cottey regained his tough demeanor. He'd had all of this grilling that he was going to put up with. He pushed forward menacingly, putting his face just inches from Carl's. "Boy, don't you threaten me with nothin'. You got somethin', you come right out with it."

"I got it put away safe." He took a step back. "It's your knife, isn't it?"

Without another word, Cottey raised his hands and lunged for Carl's throat. The younger man sidestepped easily and backed away.

Vera rushed between them. "Daddy! Stop. *Stop.*"

"You get outta here, you damned house nigger." Cottey gestured wildly at Carl, who by this time had retreated off the porch. "'Fore I kill you."

"Papa." Vera grabbed her father's thick arms. "Stop. It's Carl Tatum. Don't hurt him."

Carl continued to backpedal away from the house. "You're not helping yourself, Cottey."

"Shut up, you slave boy! Go on back to your bosses 'fore I get my shotgun."

"Daddy, *please*," Vera crooned, holding onto his arms.

He dug deep for all the bravado he could find. "Don't you threaten me, you damned old moonshiner."

"I ain't *threatenin'*, boy!"

The old outlaw broke away from Vera and disappeared back into the house. Vera rushed off the porch and tried to get Carl to leave—immediately.

"Hurry, sugar," she said, wild-eyed. "*Run.* He goin' to get that gun."

"He won't shoot me." Carl didn't believe his own words.

"Oh, yes he will, baby. Now, please, go. Hurry."

"He can't threaten me."

"Go on, Carl," Vera pleaded. "I'll see you sometime soon. You go on now. Stay out of these things. These are bad men. They'll kill you for nothin', baby. Go on, now. Go."

Carl finally let logic and Vera's entreaties convince him to go, but he would not run. He walked away, not exactly at a saunter, but as slowly as he could, trying to seem casual. Just as he reached the first nearby corner, Henry Cottey came hustling back out onto his front porch with a long, double barrel .12 gauge shotgun. He was so angry, though, he couldn't get the shells into the barrel. Vera made it doubly difficult by actively interfering with her father's loading attempt.

"Daddy, stop it!" The young woman slapped at the buckshot shells. "Stop it right now. Ain't you done enough? Carl done gone nohow."

"Get back outta my way, girl." Cottey tried to load the weapon and push Vera away at the same time.

"Stop! Stop this instant."

Thanks to Vera's interference and his own rage, the old man couldn't get the shotgun loaded until Carl had made it safely out of range. Impotent, all he could do was raise his fist and shout down the empty street. "Run, you coward bastard! You better run!"

THE CHIEF GOES TO A BALLGAME

Chief Ned Patton sat by himself in the bleachers at the Jefferson ballpark watching the local nine play against a team from Monett, Missouri. The Monett team, identified by a large green M emblazoned across the chest of their dirty, once white uniforms, was in the field. While the chief took in the game, he munched from a large bag of peanuts. Pieces of empty shells gathered around and on the chief's newly-shined police shoes.

On the diamond, Calvin, the scrappy little utility player who had found a place in the Redbirds lineup because of Ace Cooper's demise, was at bat and after taking a couple of roundhouse curveballs that missed the plate, got the fastball he was hoping for and ripped a sharp line drive single to left field. The small hometown crowd cheered happily.

"Atta boy, Calvin," Chief Patton called out supportively. "That's the way to do it."

From the home team dugout below him, Chief Patton could hear Fred Casey, the Jefferson Redbirds manager, call out to Calvin on the field.

"One away, Calvin," the skipper reminded his impulsive player. "Go hard on a ground ball."

"I'm on it, Fred."

As the chief leaned back in the stands and stretched his thick frame, Wade Smith suddenly appeared over his left shoulder. Smith sat down in back of the chief but leaned forward so that they could speak without being overheard.

Smith bypassed any preliminary greeting. "Gotta talk, Patton."

"I'm watchin' the ball game." Not bothering to turn around, the policeman nonchalantly shelled a couple of peanuts and tossed them into his mouth.

Smith hissed in the chief's ear. "That boy you got workin' for you is gonna be trouble if you don't rein him in."

The chief still refused to look at him. "Boy I got workin' for me?"

"Don't play dumb, Patton. You know who I mean. That Carl Tatum boy."

"Oh." The chief smiled, though Smith couldn't see it. "He's no problem."

"He's gonna be a problem. If he don't stop nosin' 'round."

"You worry too much."

Out on the field, a Jefferson batter had popped up to shortstop for the second out of the inning. There was a brief chorus of boos, followed by Manager Casey's standard exhortation to his next batter, Rucker.

"Come on Rucker, boy!" He slapped his hands together. "Bring that little duck in off the pond."

Rucker strode confidently to the plate from the on-deck circle, a once chalky white sphere now nearly obliterated by dirt swirled across it from countless cleats stepping over, around, and through its round form.

Up in the bleachers Wade Smith continued to harangue Chief Patton.

"Laugh it off if you want, Chiefie. You can fall as hard and as far as anybody else. And I ain't goin' down this time—not by myself anyways."

Patton sighed. "Stop frettin', son. It's all right."

"All right?" Smith snorted. "How do you make that out? Don't you realize all roads lead to you, Buster."

"Listen, Smith." The chief at last turned partially around to address his interlocutor. "I appreciate your concern, but it's okay. The roads do not lead to me. It's taken care of."

Smith looked confused. "Taken care of?"

"That's right."

"Well, I don't know what you're talkin' about." Smith shook his head. "But don't say I didn't tell you. You should have never let that boy into this in the first place. You're just askin' for trouble. I'm beginnin' to think you're soft on them people or something."

Chief Patton ignored the attempt to race bait him and concentrated again on the game where Rucker, uncharacteristically, hit a weak ground ball to second base and was easily thrown out at first base to end the inning. The visiting Monett team jogged off the field as the Jefferson players gathered themselves to replace them on the diamond. Manager Casey exhorted his charges again.

"That's all right, boys," Fred said in as upbeat a tone as he could muster. "We'll get 'em next time. Get after 'em, fellows."

The Redbirds hustled out onto the field to a smattering of perhaps ironic applause. In the bleachers, Wade Smith finished his colloquy with Chief Patton.

"Don't say I didn't warn you."

"Duly noted." The chief turned away from Smith and again casually shelled another couple of peanuts.

Smith rose and stomped off, mumbling to himself angrily. "Damned fool. I ain't goin' down. Not by myself. Not this time."

ANOTHER VISIT IN OTIS CARTER'S PASTURE

Carl Tatum and Otis Carter stood by Otis's pasture fence, feeding handfuls of fresh pulled grass to Otis's horses. Their surroundings could not have appeared more bucolic. The green pasture, verdant and full, the pleasant, tree-filled neighborhood, the blue sky above dotted with small, cottony cumulus clouds all bespoke of a tranquil, uncomplicated, and calm world. But Carl had come to Otis not for a pleasant visit in a comfortable, almost rural setting. He had sought out his older and trusted friend for some last minute advice on how to deal with what had now become a rather complicated and ticklish situation regarding the death of Robert "Ace" Cooper.

Carl knew he had to take what he had learned to the police but nothing about the situation made him feel comfortable in doing so. Otis sensed the young man's discomfort and waited for him to open the conversation. When Carl was not forthcoming, the older man finally took a deep breath, exhaled, and initiated the talk.

"It's a beautiful day." Otis hoped the trivial observation might at least get Carl to open up.

"Yes, sir." But Carl barely looked around at the world beyond the fenced-in pasture.

"Troubles got you, son?"

"Yes, sir, Mr. Carter, sir."

"Well, sometimes it's best to let them old troubles out. Keep you from explodin' at the wrong place or the wrong time."

"I know who killed that white baseball player."

"Uh-huh." Otis nodded, giving the younger man the lead.

"Well, it don't appear to be who I thought it was."

"No?"

Carl reached down to pick up a small rock, tossed it out toward the dirt road off to their right. "No, sir. I was sure it was those white moonshiners. You know, that Smith fellow and some of his bunch."

"Now you not so sure?"

The boy shook his head. "No. I'm not."

Otis fed some more grass to one of his horses and rubbed the animal along its front shoulder. "Is it pointin' back at our people?"

"Damned Patton." Carl sighed. "Lord, I hate for him to be right on this."

Otis looked across the pasture at a spot in his fence that needed mending. "Even so."

"What do I do, Mr. Carter?" He was more pleading than wondering.

"Tell the truth, son." Otis lifted his working straw hat and rubbing his thinned out white hair. "Just be straightforward. Don't let what you want to be the truth get in the way of what is true."

He shrugged. "I'm not sure."

Otis raised a finger in warning. "And if I guess as to who it may be—and I reckon I got a pretty good idea—you in danger either way you go, young Carl. Walk easy on this here one. You treadin' between a copperhead and a cottonmouth, if you get my meaning. Go light."

"I—"

But the old man wasn't finished. "Just remember. Go with the truth. In the end, it's all a man has. It's the only thing that's ever gonna save us. Any of us. All of us."

Carl stood silent for a few moments pondering Otis's words. As usual, the older horseman made a lot of sense. Seemed to understand what the right thing to do was. Finally, Carl grinned and reached out to shake Otis's hand. The older man offered his hand with a paternal smile.

"Thank you, Mr. Carter," Carl said, his shoulders straight with obvious resolution. "You're a real friend. Now wish me luck. First thing in the morning, it all comes out."

"You'll be fine, son." Otis patted his arm affectionately. "Just tell the truth. You'll be fine."

CARL GOES UPTOWN

A little before nine a.m. on the morning after Carl Tatum had his chat with Otis Carter, the young man made his way uptown. He was on a mission to report what he had learned about the death of Robert "Ace" Cooper to Chief Ned Patton at the Jefferson police station. As he walked up a narrow sidewalk leading to the city square, he was completely unaware that Henry Cottey lay in wait for him in an alley just a half block from the city center and just a few feet ahead of where Carl strode purposefully on his mission.

As Carl neared the little side alley, Cottey drew a long knife from his pants and prepared to attack. So intent was the old man on his intended victim that he failed to watch his own back and suddenly, appearing from nowhere, Otis popped out of a doorway further back down the alley and with two large steps reached Cottey and grabbed him from behind. The two men wrestled for a moment but with one powerful motion, Otis disarmed Cottey and, then, spinning the big moonshiner around, dropped him cold with a hard punch to the face.

Otis drug Cottey into another doorway just as Carl walked past the alley and the would be lawyer walked on towards the square, unaware that he had narrowly missed being injured or killed and that he'd been saved by his friend and mentor Otis Carter.

Focused completely on what he had to say and do at the police station, Carl continued on uptown, across the square past the post office, and then on below downtown to the Jefferson police station near city hall. To his surprise there was a fair-sized crowd already formed around the entrance to the station.

Picking his way through the throng, he found Chief Patton standing near the station door talking to Walt Harrison, the local newspaperman who, when he wasn't reporting on sports, covered regular news beats as well. Unable to keep the news that he himself had, Carl tried to interrupt the chief's interview with the amiable reporter.

"Chief Patton, pardon me. I've got to talk to you."

The chief kept right on talking to Harrison and Carl tried again.

"Chief, it's important. We've got to talk."

"Can't you see I'm busy with Mr. Harrison here, Carl?" The chief frowned dismissively.

"I've got to talk to you, Chief. *Now.*"

"Pardon me a moment, will you, Walt?" The chief shook his head and sighed in annoyance. "Seems this boy insists on talkin' to me. I've got to see what it is that he has to say that's so all fired important."

"That's okay, Chief." Harrison smiled. "You go ahead. I'll get some crowd reaction and then come back. How's that?"

"Mighty neighborly, Walt. Mighty neighborly. All right." The chief turned to Carl as Harrison walked away into the crowd to interview others. "Now what is it that you want to talk about that's so important you had to break into my newspaper interview? Not very courteous of you, I'd say."

"I'm sorry, Chief. But it's about the Ace Cooper murder."

"Well—"

"You have to listen to me, Chief." Carl rushed ahead, refusing to be brushed off. "I know who did it. I can prove it."

"Carl—"

"It was Henry Cottey, Chief. I thought it was white moonshiners, but then I found this knife with dried blood on it and the initials HC scratched on the blade. I was looking in the wrong place for the killer. I was—"

"Now, Carl, hold up there. Just a minute."

Carl shook his head. "No, Chief. I'm certain of it. I confronted Henry Cottey. He threatened me, he's the—"

"Carl! *Carl!*" The chief nearly had to scream to get the younger man's attention. "Listen to me now. I know you worked hard on this. And you did a real good job. But we already found our man."

"It was Henry." Carl was so sure of his own case that he was simply not hearing the words the chief was saying. Finally, after a moment or so, the sense of the situation began to settle in on him.

"It was what? What did you say?"

"I said we already got the killer." Chief Patton smiled patiently. "He was right under our noses all the time."

"You got him inside?" Carl looked around the area wildly, expecting to see Cottey in custody. But there was no one there who appeared to be under arrest. At least not there outside the police station.

"Not yet." He spoke to Carl like he would to a small child. "Patrolman Davis should be bringing in the guilty man any minute now."

"Patrolman Davis?" He didn't remember any Patrolman Davis.

"He's a new boy," the chief elaborated. "I just hired him a couple of days ago. He's out of Missouri. Nice young fellow. Be a real asset to the department."

"I don't understand. What are you talking about? Who is this Davis is bringing in? Where is he?"

"Calm down. They should be here in no time. We don't expect the guilty party to put up much of a fuss."

"Guilty party? Who is that?"

"Hold your horses. Here they come right now."

Carl, the chief, and the growing crowd turned to look back up the street towards downtown as a Jefferson patrol car crossed the southwest corner of the square and pulled up in front of the police station, facing what would have been oncoming traffic if the crowd had not already closed off the street. The arriving vehicle forced everyone either forward onto the sidewalk or back into and across the street as it came to a stop directly in front of the building.

After a brief pause, the door of the police car swung open and a tall, thin, crisply uniformed man got out. It was newly hired Patrolman Harold Davis and the sharply dressed patrolman stepped back alongside the vehicle and opened the driver's side back door.

"Come on out of there, fellow." Davis said to his passenger.

"Here's the killer of Ace Cooper," Patton called out above the crowd noise.

A noticeable gasp ran through the crowd and with them Carl and the chief watched as Patrolman Davis helped a handcuffed man out of the back seat of the police car. Someone in the crowd cried out:

"Roy Holmes!"

There was a loud stir among the watchers and Carl, without realizing it himself, repeated the name out loud.

Suddenly, emerging from the milling crowd, which was getting louder by the moment, Wanda Jeter stepped forward. She cursed Holmes roundly.

"You bastard," the grieving girlfriend cried out. "You killed my Robert. You filthy, no-good man."

Walt Harrison grabbed Wanda and restrained her from trying to actually strike Holmes. Holmes himself, crazy-eyed with fear and anger, was led by Patrolman Davis onto the sidewalk and up a short flight of concrete steps towards the station door.

As soon as Harrison felt Wanda calming down, he went into reporter mode again and began taking pictures of Holmes, the flashbulbs from his camera popping brightly even in the daylight. On the steps of the police station, Roy Holmes made an impassioned plea to the chief.

"Chief," the handcuffed ex-patrolman cried. "What are they doing? What did I do? Chief, stop them. What did I do to you? Why me?"

"Roy Holmes." Carl shook his head in complete amazement, as if he were in a bad dream from which he couldn't awake. "If that don't beat all."

At that moment, Holmes looked over and saw Carl standing there. The arrested ex-patrolman lunged for him but Patrolman Davis corralled Holmes physically. The new patrolman could not, however, stop the invective that burst from the restrained man's mouth.

"Carl Tatum! You black son of a bitch. This is your doin'. You done this to me. You always hated me."

"I never did nothin' to you, Roy." Shocked by Holmes's personal attack, he didn't know what else to say. "I know you didn't do it."

Holmes was too frantic to hear Carl's denial and so overcome by his own predicament that his attention quickly shifted to the crowd in general and he became concerned with heaping threats onto them as well.

"I'll get all of you bastards," Holmes yelled at the jeering mob. "You'll all pay. You can't do this to me. I never done nothin' to nobody. You can't—I never. I'll see you all in hell."

"Get him inside," Chief Patton told Patrolman Davis over the crowd noise. "Now. And shut him up."

"Damn you, Patton," Holmes bawled at the chief. "Damn your eyes."

The chief motioned to Davis. "Get him out of here."

Patrolman Davis struggled briefly with Holmes but then managed to get the wildly agitated former patrolman into the police station. With the object of its interest and wrath gone, the excited crowd began to quiet down and things calmed some. Carl Tatum stood off to one side of the main group as if he were in a daze. He barely heard Chief Patton as the policeman tried to break up the gathering.

"Show's over, folks," Patton's voice boomed over the heads of what was left of the crowd. "Break it up now. Time to go home. Nothin' left here to see."

The crowd did slowly disperse then, but not without some grumbling. Walt Harrison detached himself from the last of the crowd and approached the chief in hopes of getting more information about the arrest of Roy Holmes.

"Chief?" The reporter hustled over with his camera in one hand and a pad and pencil in the other, the very picture of journalistic sincerity.

"Give us just a little bit, will you, Walt?"

"Sure, Chief."

Patton turned to Carl. "Quite a day, ain't it, Tatum? Really great."

"I ain't so sure, sir." Carl shook his head.

"Aw, now, don't think like that. You done good, son. No doubt about it. You did just fine and now your work is done. We won't be needin' you anymore. But next week, you come by the station. I'll have a little somethin' for you. That's certain. A little something."

"Yeah, sure." Still thrown by the unexpected turn of events., Carl wasn't ready to talk. "Next week. Something."

"This ought to shut up Tommy Ball and that Clean Government League bunch for awhile, huh?" Chief Patton clapped him on the shoulder as if they were the best of friends. "It all worked out real clean. Just right."

"Just right?"

"Why, hell, boy, Holmes is the one that shot at you a few days back there. You should be happy we got him. You're safe now."

"Safe?"

"You bet safe."

"Chief," Carl regained some of his normal clarity of thought, "even if it was Holmes that shot at me, that don't make him the killer."

"Oh, he's the one, all right. Don't you worry about that. We got our man, that's for sure."

"But sir—" He could not believe how illogical this arrest was. All his work was being co-opted by some sort of ruse put on by Chief Patton. "There's just no way."

The chief was not interested in his ideas or his proof, though. The lawman had had all the conversation he wanted for the time being.

"That's enough of that talk, son," Chief Patton said, not unkindly. "You take care now, Carl. And be sure and come see us next week. I mean it. I'll have somethin' for you. Now I gotta go on. We be seein' you."

With that pronouncement, the chief hitched up his pistol belt and with an obvious air of self-satisfaction strolled happily back towards the front doors of the police station. Walt Harrison looked up from his writing and saw the chief leaving. With a little yelp, he hurried after the chief, camera and notepad at the ready.

As for Carl, he simply could not believe the way in which the murder investigation had so abruptly and so oddly concluded. There was no way on

God's green earth that Roy Holmes was the killer of Ace Cooper. Carl had proved that, confronted the killer, and come downtown with his evidence to show the police. And then Chief Ned Patton, always an unknown and not fully understood quantity in the equation, had decided of his own accord to put the blame on one of his own officers.

It was a move he chastised himself for not being able to see ahead of time. But how could he have? He had solved the murder pure and clean and now the chief was arbitrarily choosing to subvert the logical and legal basis of the entire case. Carl knew that Roy Holmes, as a pesky little punk of a policeman, was an annoyance to all the citizens of Jefferson but Ned Patton's arrest of the patrolman spoke of hidden conflicts and unseen, unspoken motivations that he was not privy to.

He thought of Dinty Blaine and how the old man assiduously avoided the problems of white people and of how Otis Carter had warned him of the white power base solving its own problems without heed to nor recompense for the nearly invisible black community of Jefferson.

With these thoughts in mind, Carl began to walk slowly back up towards the square. He was feeling pretty low. Then suddenly, out of nowhere, Tommy Ball popped out of a doorway near the square and hustled up to him.

"Congratulations." Tommy thrust out his hand.

"For what?" He was surprised—not just by Tommy's sudden appearance, but by his enthusiastic greeting and energized attitude as well.

"For bringing down one of the really bad guys. What else?"

"You mean Roy Holmes? He didn't kill Ace Cooper."

Ball shook his head. "It doesn't matter. Holmes is one of them. Was. Patton gave us a sacrifice. He knows he's losing his grip on Jefferson. His power, with his brother and those others of their kind, has been weakened. We've won a big one here."

"Don't much look like that to me, Mr. Ball."

"Oh, we didn't knock the house down. I'll grant you that. But we shook it up. And good. Next time it falls. And you're a big part of that."

"Hmph. Next time? When exactly would that next time be?"

Tommy ignored his questions. "The city, through those of us on the council who appreciate you, will vote you some money for the work you did, too."

"Blood money," Carl said heatedly. "Lie money. Patton already offered it. What I learned was just swept under the carpet, tossed away."

"Don't think of it that way. Things don't always work out so clean and easy. But you helped a lot. Take the money offered to you. At least take it to help your family. What about your mama and papa?"

Carl considered that point for a moment. Anything would help him and his family during this very, very difficult era. "Yes. It would help my folks."

"Atta, boy." Tommy Ball slapped him on the arm. "And don't forget, I'm still workin' on your bar exam application. It's gonna happen. Someday, and soon. This is goin' to be your town, too. You'll see."

Carl's gaze turned dark. "This already is my town, Mr. Ball, just as much as it is Chief Patton's, or the mayor's, or yours. Or anybody's."

"All right. That's the spirit. Come see me soon." With that Tommy broke off the conversation and headed on down the hill towards the police station and the city council offices.

Carl silently watched him go, then continued on his way up to and through the square. Otis Carter was waiting for him on the far east side beyond the post office.

"Why so glum?"

Carl couldn't keep the sneer off his face. "Did you hear?"

"I heard. It spread through town faster than a grass fire on the prairie."

"Can it get any worse?"

"Oh, I've seen it a sight worse." Otis shook his gray head.

He sighed. "And now I gotta watch all the time for Henry Cottey."

"Leave Henry to me. He won't be botherin' you as long as I'm around. You needn't trouble yourself about that." Carl gave Otis an odd, not-understanding look, but said nothing. "That's all taken care of."

"What did you do?"

"You never mind about that. Just don't fret about Henry Cottey. That's all."

"Thank you, Mr. Carter."

Otis shrugged. "Nothin' to it."

"But nothing's really changed." Carl paused. "And that poor, dumb Roy Holmes didn't have nothin' to do with this crime. Patton just sacrificed him to take all the pressure off himself."

Otis shurgged. "It was their way of workin' out their own differences. Chief get somethin', Tommy Ball get somethin', mayor get somethin'. It was just white folks fussin' with one another. They all got what they wanted."

"I suppose so. But what did we get? What did I get?"

"You get to know that you were in the right," Otis told his young friend. "That you learned the truth. On your own. And you faced it and did the right thing. It takes a special man to do that."

He was unconvinced, though. "I guess that's something."

"You bet it is. And because you did it, it's for all of us, too."

"It just seems like that ain't enough somehow. You know?"

"I do know." Otis nodded. "But there's bigger things at work here. The sun'll come up in the mornin' and it'll be shinin' on a better man. That's you. And maybe a little bit better of a town here, too. You'll see."

"Maybe so."

"Things are goin' to get better, son." Otis put his arm around Carl's shoulders. "I know they will. For all the folks in Jefferson."

"Yes, sir." Carl stood up tall and straight. "It will get better. I'm gonna take their blood money for my family and I'm gonna take their damned old bar exam. They're not going to stop me forever. And then all of our folks are going to have somebody on their side. All the poor folks."

"That's the way to talk. And you can do it, too."

"Yes, I can."

"We all mighty proud of you, son."

"Thank you, sir. I mean to do the best I can for all of us."

Otis smiled. "You bet."

He let out a big sigh and managed a smile of his own. Otis patted the young man on the shoulder again. "Now, what you say. You hungry? I believe I could do with a bit of food after all this excitement."

He nodded. "Lord, I'm starvin', Mr. Carter. I didn't even realize."

"Well come on, then. Let's go down to Ola Mae's and git her and Dinty to make us up a big old hungry man's breakfast. What do you say?"

"Sounds mighty fine to me. Lead the way."

"Okay," Otis agreed. "Let's go, but together."

"You bet." He smiled. "Together."

"That's the way to do it," Otis told his young friend. "That's the way."

The two men walked on proudly then, side by side, across the square and down towards Tin Hollow. On through town, towards home, towards the future.

www.ingramcontent.com/pod-product-compliance
Lightning Source LLC
Chambersburg PA
CBHW022128170626
46808CB00002B/895